Tales From The Annals of Sherlock Holmes

Arthur Hall

First edition published in 2021

Paperback ISBN 978-1-78705-696-1

ePub ISBN 978-1-78705-697-8

PDF ISBN 978-1-78705-698-5

MX Publishing

335 Princess Park Manor, Royal Drive,

London, N11 3GX

www.mxpublishing.com

Cover design by Brian Belanger

Arthur Hall was born in Aston, Birmingham, UK, in 1944. His interest in writing began during his schooldays and served as a growing ambition to become an author.

Years later, his first novel 'Sole Contact' was an espionage story about an ultra-secret government department known as 'Sector Three' and has been followed, to date, by five sequels.

Other works include five 'rediscovered' cases from the files of Sherlock Holmes, two collections of bizarre short stories and two novels about an adventurer called 'Bernard Kramer', as well as several contributions to the ongoing anthology, 'The MX Book of New Sherlock Holmes Stories'.

His only ambition, apart from being published more widely, is to attend the premier of a film based on one of his novels, ideally at The Odeon, Leicester Square.

He lives in the West Midlands, United Kingdom, where he often walks other people's dogs as he attempts to formulate new plots.

His work can be seen at: arthurhallsbooksite.blogspot.com, and the author can be contacted at: arthurhall7777@aol.co.uk

By the same author:

The 'Sector Three' series:

Sole Contact

A Faint and Distant Threat

The Final Strategy

The Plain Face of Truth

A Certain Way to Death

The Suicide Chase

The 'Bernard Kramer' series:

The Sagittarius Ring

Controlled Descent

Sci-fi and weird short stories:

Facets of Fantasy

Curious Tales

Rediscovered cases from the files of Sherlock Holmes:

The Demon of the Dusk

The One Hundred per Cent Society

The Secret Assassin

The Phantom Killer

In Pursuit of the Dead

Further Little-Known Cases of Sherlock Holmes

Contents:

The Adventure of the Exalted Victim

As I sit, here in our rooms in Baker Street, recording some of my extraordinary experiences as the friend and colleague of Mr Sherlock Holmes, it occurs to me that many of our adventures began within these walls. But this was not always so. One exception that comes to mind is the curious affair of Mr Wallace Abrahams and his unfortunate brother, which I will attempt to relate here from my notes and the vestiges of my recollection.

We had visited Lestrade at Scotland Yard, on Holmes' insistence. For once it was my friend who congratulated the inspector, on his successful handling of the case that sent Kirkby to the gallows.

'You did well, Lestrade, he was a particularly brutal murderer.'

'The difficult part of it all was proving that Kirkby was in London at the time, ' the little detective said. 'He had half a dozen witnesses who swore that he drank with them in a pub in Brighton that same night.'

'The witnesses were so adamant that I doubted that their testimony was bought,' Holmes recollected. 'When you requested my assistance, my first act was to examine the official records to ensure that Kirkby had no twin or close relative of similar appearance. Finding none, I journeyed to Brighton and eventually discovered a local stage actor of small parts who looked enough like our man to have needed no more than a little make-up to complete the deception.'

Lestrade nodded. 'Your help saved me from much embarrassment, Mr Holmes, as well as preventing a guilty man from cheating the law. One thing has always puzzled me, though.'

Holmes brought his gaze back from a study of the inspector's office ceiling. 'Pray tell me. I will enlighten you if I can.'

'When the actor was brought to London to be charged as an accessory, we saw how close the resemblance was. Yet you had no difficulty in telling the two men apart, at any time. How were you able to do this?'

'This mystified me also.' I remarked.

'There really is no mystery about it,' Holmes gave one of his quick, patient smiles. 'Did either of you notice a peculiarity in Kirkby's mode of dress?'

Lestrade and I glanced at each other, and then it came to me. 'Kirkby never wore a cravat. He tried a scarf around his neck.'

'Excellent, Watson. You will recall that the actor, Murton, dressed similarly to aid the prosecution's case in demonstrating that one man could be substituted for the other. He had been promised leniency, for doing so.'

'I remember,' said Lestrade.

'Then the difference becomes clear, does it not, when we remember also that Murton was formerly a naval man. He tied his scarf in another fashion, a seaman's knot.'

'It seems to me that it should be I congratulating you,' Lestrade said. 'All that was left for me was the arrest.'

'Thus adding one more to your considerable record.' Holmes picked up his hat and got to his feet.

At that moment the desk sergeant appeared in the doorway.

'This gentleman insists on seeing you, Inspector Lestrade.'

A small man, I estimated him to be in his mid-sixties, was ushered in as we took our leave. He removed his bowler, and I saw that he was completely bald save for his thick side-whiskers and magnificent handlebar moustache. Holmes and I wished him good morning as we passed, and Lestrade invited him to be seated.

#

The following morning I sat reading one of the early editions, as Holmes stared wistfully from the window. Mrs Hudson had cleared away our breakfast things, before he finally spoke.

'Have the brandy decanter ready, Watson.'

'It is a little early for me, Holmes.'

'Of that I have no doubt, but the poor fellow who is about to visit us may benefit from a glass. He is in a highly excitable state, and we have already made his acquaintance, briefly.'

I poured the drink and kept it in readiness, and a few minutes later a quick exchange at the door was followed by a noisy ascent before our good lady showed in the gentleman who we had left with Lestrade yesterday.

'Mr Wallace Abrahams, to see Mr Holmes,' she announced before withdrawing.

'My dear fellow,' Holmes began. 'I see that you are in some distress. Sit with us here and take a glass of brandy to calm your nerves before telling us how we can assist you.'

Our visitor obeyed gladly and gulped the spirit down. As he replaced the glass on the tray, a puzzled look came into his eyes.

Holmes realised his difficulty at once. 'Forgive me for not introducing ourselves, Mr Abrahams. I am Sherlock Holmes, and this is my friend and colleague Doctor John Watson who you may speak to with the same confidence as you would to myself.'

Mr Abrahams recovered himself slightly, and looked from Holmes to me and back again. 'Thank you, gentlemen. You may recall that we met briefly in Inspector Lestrade's office, yesterday.'

'Indeed we did. Is it the same matter that brings you here today?'

'It is, Mr Holmes, and I am desperate.'

'Was Lestrade unwilling or unable to assist you, then?' My friend enquired.

'He tried sir. He said I was probably mistaken, that grief can do that to a man, and he sent constables to the house but they found it empty.'

'I think,' said Holmes, 'that we are approaching this from the wrong direction. Pray take a moment to reflect, and then tell us all from the beginning. A little more brandy, perhaps?'

The little man shook his head, and then realised that he still wore his hat and removed it. 'My apologies, and no more to drink thank you, sirs. What I am about to tell you is a story hard to believe, but I need a clear head to tell it all the same.'

'Then if you are ready, pray proceed.'

'I think you know already that my name is Wallace Abrahams. I am fortunate that I am retired from work.'

'I had gathered as much.'

The puzzled expression returned to our visitor's face. 'How did you know that , sir?'

'The condition of your hands tells me that you did manual labour for some years, but the surface of the skin now appears smooth, revealing that the work has ceased. You are obviously no longer a young man, so retirement was a natural conclusion.'

'Why, that is extraordinary, that you should see that.' Mr Abrahams smiled for the first time. 'I worked on the railways, laying track and dragging those wooden sleepers. I saved every penny that I could. I never married, never met the right woman. When his wife died, five years ago, Garland came to live with me in the house I bought.'

'Garland is your brother? I enquired.

'He is, or was,' his face fell, presumably as he was reminded of his troubles. 'Now, after all this – I cannot be sure.'

Holmes looked at him thoughtfully. 'Please enlighten us, as to this most curious situation.'

'One month ago,' Mr Abrahams put his head in his hands and spoke in a trembling voice, 'I returned home to Clapham in the late afternoon. The road I lived in was usually quiet, being in the Old Town and not far from the Common, but that day it was clogged with fire brigade carts and people wanting to see what was going on. I turned a corner and saw to my horror that it was my house that was ablaze, and as I watched a fireman carried out the charred remains of Garland. Then came a shower of sparks as the roof fell in.'

'So you were left without shelter,' I observed.

'No, I was fortunate in having another house nearby, a small place that I often let out. At that time it was vacant and so I moved there, to be alone with my grief. Then, yesterday, I walked through Clapham, I had taken to wandering aimlessly for hours, and I passed a house with turrets like a castle. As I walked by, the great double doors opened and four men came out. With them, to my astonishment, was Garland, as alive and well as we are sitting here now. I could not believe my eyes. I made to approach him to ensure that I was not mistaken or going mad but one of his companions, a huge bearded brute, pushed me roughly aside and said in a harsh foreign accent, 'If you interfere, we will kill you. Make no mistake.'

Holmes looked up thoughtfully. 'Did you recognise any of the men accompanying your brother?'

'I am certain that I had never seen any of them before.'

'Did your brother appear to recognise you?'

'He had a look of terror and, I thought, of abject hopelessness. A coach swept them away then, and I could do nothing.'

'Did you notice anything else unusual about him?'

Our client considered. 'A small thing. I suppose it has no significance.'

'It is my experience that small things often have much significance.'

'Well, it was just that Garland was unshaven. For him that is unheard of, for he has always been most particular about all aspects of his appearance.'

'That is highly significant. From there you went to Scotland Yard?'

'I did, and the outcome was as I have mentioned. When nothing was found at the house I asked Inspector Lestrade if anything more could be done. At first he asked me to seriously consider whether I could have been mistaken, and when I replied that I was quite certain that my brother was alive although I had seen his burnt body, he said that if I believed there was any mystery here I should consult you. He then gave me your address.'

'That was most kind of the good inspector.'

There was a moment of silence, except for the sound of a trotting horse outside, as

Mr Abrahams sat very still, seemingly full of nervous anticipation.

It was impossible to read Holmes' expression, but I knew that his mind would be racing.

'I have only a few more questions, Mr Abrahams, then I will bid you good day,' he said at last. 'I will most certainly look into this and let you know the results. Firstly, at your brother's funeral, did you notice anything out of the ordinary?'

Our visitor's relief at gaining Holmes' help was evident as he said, after some little thought: 'Only that the minister, the Reverend Potter who I am acquainted with, was replaced by a priest I had never seen before. The reason was never explained, nor has Reverend Potter been seen since. There is another priest there now.'

'Did this replacement priest, by any chance, have a foreign accent?'

'He had a strange accent, certainly, but I could not tell if it was foreign.'

'Was it, for example, anything like that of the man who prevented you from speaking to your brother?'

He hesitated, then shook his head again. 'I could not be certain.'

'Very well. At what church was the funeral held?'

'It was St Thaddeus, in Clapham.'

Holmes gave me a quick glance to ensure that I was making notes.

'And finally, please describe your brother to us.'

Mr Abrahams said nothing but reached inside his coat to produce a photograph which he handed to Holmes, and I saw a strange look in my friend's eyes. In an instant it was gone, and I leaned over to see a portrait of an elderly, rather stout gentleman. He was clean-shaven, and his hair had thinned considerably above his brow. I could see no reason for Holmes' astonishment.

'May I keep this?' he asked.

'You could keep every penny that I own, if that would bring Garland back to me, Mr Holmes. He is, or was, my only remaining relative.'

'Fortunately, that will not be necessary,' my friend smiled. 'You will hear from me soon.'

Mr Abrahams made to rise, but stopped. 'Forgive me, I have quite forgotten to tell you the other side of this.'

'There is something more?'

'There is, and I should have told you at the beginning. Since my encounter with the men who were with Garland in Clapham, I have been followed by one or other of them. I thought I was imagining this at first, but now I am sure.'

'This changes the picture considerably,' Holmes said as he got to his feet. 'We will accompany you to your home, and see what move they make.'

#

I was able to summon a passing hansom, and we were soon on our way. Holmes looked in every direction, as did I, but we saw nothing as we joined the heavy traffic.

'Aha!' he exclaimed as we progressed along Baker Street, and I peered back to see a man in a long black coat frantically attempting to attract the attention of a coach driver who was setting down a fare on the opposite side of the road.

'We shall see if we can make things a little more difficult for him.' Holmes rapped the roof with his stick, telling the driver to take the next turn and directing him through a maze of side-streets.

By the time we reached Mr Abraham's house, a three-storey red brick building in a quiet tree-lined street on the outskirts of Clapham, we were certain that our pursuer had not reappeared.

'It will be best if we enter with you to inspect the premises,' Holmes advised.

'But what do you expect to find?'

'I wish to be certain that our adversaries have not been here before us, or are concealed within. Be in no doubt that your life is in danger, Mr Abrahams. We must test every step in our investigation before we commit ourselves.'

'I am not sure that I understand you,'

The hansom rattled away, taking a different return route on Holmes' instruction, before he answered.

'Firstly, I am not at all convinced that you were not being followed, long before you were aware of it.'

'I suppose that is possible.'

'Indeed it is likely. I suspect that those holding your brother prisoner are threatening to kill you in order to be sure of his co-operation, although you were not meant to know this. Also, remember what was said to you when you encountered them.'

'But to what end?'

'I am unsure, as of now. My theory has yet to be proven.'

We entered the house and I remained in the hall with Mr Abrahams, while Holmes checked every room. When this was over he called to us to join him on the first floor, and we climbed the steep stairs cautiously.

'This window,' he indicated, 'gives an excellent view of the area immediately outside your front door. I recommend that you use it to view any callers, and do not admit anyone, even a uniformed constable, other than Inspector Lestrade, Doctor Watson or myself. I will ask Lestrade if he can spare a man to watch the house, but not approach.'

'Thank you, Mr Holmes,' he glanced at me. 'No, thank you both.'

'I need hardly remind you,' Holmes said, 'to ensure that all outer doors and windows are locked at all times, until this affair is over. Good day, Mr Abrahams, you will hear from me soon.'

With that we left him. A brisk walk took us to the centre of Clapham, where Holmes despatched a telegram.

'That was to Lestrade?' I ventured as he rejoined me outside the Post Office.

'No, to Mycroft.'

'Your brother is somehow connected to this case?'

Holmes raised his hand as a hansom came towards us, after leaving a fare further along the street. 'Only as a source of confirmation. I believe that certain information from him could reveal to us our adversary's purpose.'

I knew better than to press him further. Experience has long taught me that Holmes will rarely confide his thoughts prematurely.

We boarded the hansom and set off for Baker Street. I turned from the window to see him with his eyes half-closed.

'Holmes, we have just passed the house that Mr Abrahams described. It must be that, for there is none other like it anywhere here. Do you not wish to examine the rooms?'

He shook his head and gave a long sigh. 'I fear that little purpose would be served, after Lestrade's men have trampled through the place like a herd of cattle. Also, you will have observed the downstairs windows being adorned with new curtains, telling us that the owner has already re-let the house and that any clues will almost certainly have been obscured.'

We said nothing more, Holmes sitting with his head on his chest as was his custom when he was unravelling a case, until we reached our lodgings. Mrs Hudson had prepared a sumptuous lunch of roast lamb with mint sauce which he ate with unusual appetite. He refused the dessert of apple pie and clotted cream however, and as soon as I had finished mine he leapt from his chair.

‘Come, Watson, if you are free this afternoon you may care to accompany me back to Clapham. I have revised the direction which this investigation is to take.’

‘I am free until the end of the week, as you know, and with you of course. Are we to visit Mr Abrahams again, so soon?’

‘Not at all. There are things I must know before we proceed further, of which I can learn only at St Thaddeus.’

‘The church where Mr Abrahams’ brother’s funeral was held?’

‘Precisely.’

#

Except for two elderly ladies placing flowers on the graves of departed loved ones, the churchyard was deserted as we arrived. Holmes led the way past the lynch gate and along the gravel path to the ancient iron-studded door. It squealed like a tormented spirit as he pushed it open, admitting us to a cavernous, echoing interior.

There were two people here, one moving about in the far shadows and the other standing stiffly at the lectern, bathed in the pattern of coloured light from the stained-glass windows. I could see that this figure wore priest’s robes, which flowed around him as he became aware of us and approached. He looked at us curiously, as if about to remind us that there was no service until later in the day.

‘Can I assist you gentlemen?’

‘Good afternoon, Reverend. My name is Sherlock Holmes,’ my friend replied. ‘I would be grateful for some information.’

Recognition dawned immediately on the priest’s young and studious face. ‘The consulting detective? Yes, I have read of you, sir.' He switched his gaze to me. 'And this must be Doctor Watson, who so ably chronicles your exploits. I am pleased to meet you both, gentlemen, but how can I help?'

'I am enquiring about a funeral service that was conducted here, about a month ago.'

'Just before I commenced my work here, in fact.' The Reverend indicated that we should follow him into an alcove near the organ, where he selected a thick volume from a pile of dusty books. 'Do you have the name of the deceased?'

Holmes nodded. 'I understand that it was Mr Garland Abrahams.'

The priest whipped through the pages.

'Here it is,' he cried at last. 'The whole thing was very odd indeed, actually. I was told about it when I was sent to take over here.' He turned to us, slightly embarrassed. 'Forgive me, I should have introduced myself. I am Reverend Brookes, and I was given this parish because my predecessor, Reverend Potter, apparently abandoned his post.'

'Unusual, wouldn't you think, for a man of the cloth?'

'It is indeed,' Reverend Brookes continued, 'but there is something here more unusual still, strange, even.'

'And what is that, pray?' Holmes enquired.

'Well, and I must tell you gentlemen that I am still puzzled by this now, as are the church authorities. It seems that Reverend Potter left on the very day of Mr Abrahams's funeral, leaving no one to take the service. The service came to be administered by another priest, a Reverend Smith.'

'But why is that strange?' I asked.

Reverend Brookes spread out his hands, as if emphasising his confusion. 'Because, dear sirs, the church authorities know nothing of this man. He observed the funeral rites, though rather abruptly, and left. Some of the mourners have asked me about him because he was unfamiliar to them, but I can tell them nothing.'

This came as no surprise to me since I had already deduced, as Holmes must have done before me, that Reverend Brookes was not the priest described by Mr Wallace Abrahams: his accent was neither strange nor foreign.

'Curious indeed,' Holmes observed. 'So you, yourself, never actually met this man?'

'No, but there I can help you.' He turned and called into the shadows behind us. 'Mrs Clement! Come here for a moment, please.'

A tiny elderly lady wearing a pinafore over her dress emerged from the shadows near the altar, where it was just possible to see that she had been arranging flowers.

After introducing us and explaining our purpose, Reverend Brookes went back to his work at the lectern and Mrs Clement spoke in a low voice.

'I was here on the day of Mr Garland Abraham's funeral,' she began, 'as I have been every day, these many years. I confess to not approving of this priest who appeared unannounced, nor of his manner. Sirs, do you blame me for that, when he rushes through a sacred ritual with such disrespect?'

'Not at all,' said Holmes. 'But apart from the way he conducted himself, was there anything in particular that struck you as unusual?'

There was no hesitation. 'Two things stand out to me. You understand, gentlemen, that I am not normally what you might call an inquisitive person, but out of concern for the deceased and those grieving I was anxious that all should proceed properly.'

'Of course,' my friend assured her with a trace of impatience.

'Well, the first thing was his accent. I don't like foreigners in our churches and, although he tried to disguise it, that voice did not stem from this country.'

'I see. Tell me pray, about the other thing that you so astutely noticed.'

Her eyes glowed suddenly, in the way of someone about to disclose a secret. 'It was the coffin. That Reverend Smith hardly moved away from it. He watched it as if he were expecting Mr Abrahams to rise up out of it and come back to life. But what really puzzled me was something I overheard, accidentally you understand, in a conversation between Reverend Smith and one of the undertaker's men. Someone wanted the coffin opened so they could put something in with him, I don't know why unless it was a relative or friend wanting to leave something for sentimental reasons. His brother, the other Mr Abrahams, approved even though it was at such a late stage, but when this was put to Reverend Smith he was appalled! He shrank back against the casket as if he was protecting it, and would not continue with the burial until the idea was abandoned. He even quoted a scripture to support his actions which I swear he made up, because in all my years here I've never heard of it. What do you think of that, sirs?'

'Extraordinary!' I exclaimed.

'Most peculiar,' Holmes answered. 'However, we will take up no more of your time. You and the good Reverend Brookes have been most helpful. Good afternoon to you both.'

With that he swept us quickly away. A hansom answered his call and on our way back to Baker Street he settled into one of his long silences. I, however, could not contain my confusion any longer and risked an interruption.

'Holmes, I am puzzled by this turn of events. That the unusual accent of this mysterious priest aroused suspicion I can understand, but what of his concern for a sealed coffin?'

He raised his head from his chest. 'All his words and actions obviously reveal his anxiety that the casket should not be opened at any cost,' he said thoughtfully. 'We know that the contents cannot, if Mr Abrahams is to believed, be the remains of his brother, and must therefore have been those of someone else.'

I felt a flash of inspiration. 'Could the body of Reverend Potter have been hidden there?'

'I have considered that, and will give it my attention later. There are other possibilities, however. For example, it could be that the remains that the gang holding Mr Abraham's brother have caused to be placed there are female, possibly because no others were available quickly enough to be placed in the burning house. In that case the deception would of course have been discovered at once, if the coffin lid were removed. It seems to be essential to their plans that he is believed to have died.'

'Do you believe that the unfamiliar accent of the man who threatened Mr Abrahams in the presence of his brother, and that of this unknown priest are the same, thereby connecting these two events?'

'I have thought so since the circumstances were first explained to us.'

With that he lapsed back into his thoughts and I disturbed him no more.

#

After dinner I settled into an armchair with the evening edition of The Standard, while Holmes busied himself searching his index.

'It does not seem to have been reported,' he mused to himself. 'I must see Lestrade.'

'What are you looking for?' I asked.

He looked at me as if he had suddenly become aware of my presence. 'Sorry, old fellow, I was lost in my thoughts. In the morning I must go to Scotland Yard, and then to see Mycroft, whose reply to my telegram has summoned me to the Diogenes Club. You are welcome to accompany me, if you would care to.'

'I regret, Holmes, that I must return to my practice unexpectedly. You will recall that I also received a telegram. It was from the locum currently running my practice, and who seems to be having some sort of difficulty. I said I would call in to see him, to put matters right.'

'Of course,' he said a little disappointedly. 'If you must, you must. I hope you settle things quickly.'

'I expect to be back by mid-afternoon.'

'Capital!'.

He said no more, but spent the evening conducting experiments at his laboratory bench. When I had finished reading I decided to repair early to my bed, and he acknowledged my leaving with a distracted grunt. But I could not sleep, and heard him still working far into the night.

#

The remains of Holmes' breakfast were on the table when Mrs Hudson served mine, next morning. I arrived at my practice early and returned to Baker Street as I had predicted, by mid-afternoon. I had not yet had time to call to Mrs Hudson for tea, before the front door slammed and I heard him bound quickly up the stairs.

The door burst open and he strode in with a spring in his step.

'The day went well,' I observed.

'Indeed, and my demeanour evidently demonstrates as much.' He hung his coat and hat on the stand and at once sat down in the empty armchair, facing me across the low table.

'Shall I ring for tea?'

He took up his cherrywood pipe. 'A little later. First I must tell you what I have learned.'

I saw that this was to be one of the rare occasions when my friend would be forthcoming about his activities, and I was keen to listen.

'I am all ears, Holmes.'

'When I left here this morning, I went directly to Scotland Yard,' he began as he blew a smoke ring at the ceiling. 'I was convinced that a priest of Reverend Potter's experience would not abandon his calling in such a way, and it occurred to me that the most likely reasons for his disappearance would be if he were held prisoner or murdered.'

'Was Lestrade able to throw any light on this?'

'Sadly, he was. On the day that Mr Garland Abraham's funeral took place, a body was recovered from the Thames. Its head and limbs had been removed, and the rats had found it first, but it has been identified as that of Reverend Potter from a tattoo on its shoulder.'

'That is ghastly,' I said, reacting to the body's condition. 'But is it not strange that a priest should be tattooed?'

Holmes shook his head. 'Not in this case. Before he became a man of the cloth, Potter was a naval man like Murton, the actor. He served for years in the tropics, where tattoos are common as a protection against malaria. Apparently they act as a barrier against the disease, in some way.'

'I have heard of this, before now.'

The silence of the room was interrupted briefly by cries from the street below, and by the neighing of a passing horse. Holmes knocked out his pipe and continued:

'After telling the good inspector about our discoveries, I caught a hansom to Pall Mall. I knew that Mycroft would be at the Diogenes Club at that time of day, and I was left in the Stranger's Room while he was summoned.'

I learned forward eagerly. 'And what did you learn? Could he help?'

'Oh, yes. I now know who we are up against, and why. I do not exaggerate, Watson, when I tell you that the outcome of this will have a considerable effect on the future of the British Empire.'

I was profoundly shocked. 'Good heavens! How can this be?' Before my friend could answer, it came to me. 'Of course - the foreign accents. There is an international conspiracy involved, here!'

'Indeed. You are not wrong, even if a little late forming the correct conclusion. Our adversary is none other than Imperial

Germany, and our country is under a threat that is as yet largely unrecognised. Were it not for Mycroft, I would still have been unaware of it.'

'Then what is the next step?' I enquired. 'There must be something that we can do against them.'

'Not yet. According to my brother they cannot move for at least a month. Their actions depend on the first of a series of forthcoming events that begin then. We must wait, however much of a trial that is for us.'

A week went by, without incident. It was then that Holmes was presented with the problem that I have chronicled elsewhere as "The Disappearance of Lady Frances Carfax", but because of the persistent danger to Mr Wallace Abrahams, concerning which he would tell me no more, he was unable to leave the capital. It was therefore I who journeyed to Lausanne as his representative, only to be unexpectedly joined by him quite soon. My first question to him was of course concerning the situation that he had left behind, and his answer was that he could no longer bear to stagnate.

'But what of Abrahams?' I asked with concern. 'Is the danger past?'

'By no means,' he inhaled from his briar and blew out a swirling cloud of smoke. 'I decided that I could leave if I increased his protection adequately. Barker, the private enquiry agent who I have used before, is watching Abraham's house independently of Lestrade's men who, thanks to Mycroft's influence, continue their duty. Barker is under orders to contact me by wire, at the slightest change. Also, so that Abrahams can have some freedom and is no longer a prisoner in his own house, I have hired two prize-fighters from McMurdo who we know of old. That, I think, should suffice until we return.'

This new case progressed, and was brought to a satisfactory conclusion when the lady was saved, although Holmes' disappointment at the escape of our adversaries was written on his face. The subject soon dropped from our conversation however, once we were back in London and seated again in our familiar sitting room. Two days passed before he received a telegram from Mycroft consisting of only two words: It begins.

He passed it across the breakfast table for me to read, after which I saw on his face a deep frown of concern.

'Holmes,' I said quietly, 'is it not time that you revealed to me the true nature of this affair involving the Abrahams brothers? What is the enemy's purpose? What is it that begins soon?'

His eyes were as hard as flint when his gaze fell upon me, so that I felt that I had intruded, but they were soon to soften as his expression cleared and he replied in his most reasonable tone.

'You are quite right of course, Watson. I probably should have confided in you earlier. If there is any excuse for me, old friend, it is that I was overwhelmed by the gravity and enormity of the situation. The seed that Abrahams planted with us has grown into a mighty tree.'

'Very well, Holmes, but tell me now. Who are these German agents? What is their purpose?'

'According to Mycroft they are four of their best operators, from the same stable as Oberstein. Their leader, if I am not much mistaken, is the man who threatened Mr Wallace Abrahams, the same who has ensured that he is constantly in fear of death to ensure the co-operation of his kidnapped brother. His name, or least the one he currently uses, is Kurt Bekker.'

'Scoundrels!' I exclaimed. 'But still, I see no purpose in all this.'

Holmes nodded. 'That is easily corrected. Pray hand me the photograph of Abraham's brother, which stands on the shelf near your right arm.'

I complied, and he placed his hands so that they shielded part of the likeness. 'Now, imagine him with a full beard. Has he not now become familiar to you?'

I peered at the picture, over his shoulder. At first I saw nothing but what I had seen before, then all at once I realised the truth of it all.

'Great heavens, Holmes! He looks like…..'

'Almost a twin, wouldn't you say?'

'I would swear,' I had to pause, for it was suddenly difficult to breathe, 'that this is a likeness of ……..'

'Of The Most Honourable Robert Gascoyne-Cecil, Third Marquess of Salisbury, KG. PC. FRS. DZ.' Holmes finished. 'You could be forgiven for believing so,' a quick smile flittered across his face and was gone, 'but it is, as was represented to us, of Mr Garland Abrahams. I saw the hidden resemblance at once, at first sight of the photograph. That is why I consulted Mycroft, because the implications were immediately apparent.'

'But this is awful. Bekker and his men clearly intend to substitute this man for the Prime Minister. But why would they do this?'

'I could find no reason, despite considerable research. But again, it was Mycroft who supplied the answer. Once we were alone in the Stranger's Room, he told me all. During the next few months, members of the Spanish, Italian and French governments will visit our capital at different times. During the course of these visits each will meet the Prime Minister prior to a decision being reached on a vital and far-reaching matter. If the kidnapped Mr Abrahams were substituted, not only would Bekker and his men learn of the proceedings but they could instruct him, on pain of his brother's death, to sabotage any or all of the meetings.'

'This is monstrous. Did Mycroft confide in you the substance of the discussions?'

'Only in general terms, as far as his position would allow. Each of these foreign dignitaries is party to a plan, a treaty, that if implemented would benefit our country considerably, but would work against the interests of Imperial Germany. Clearly, Bekker and his friends have been sent to disrupt this agreement, to our detriment.'

I considered for a moment. 'Holmes, what do you suppose they intend to do to the Prime Minister, once he is in their hands?'

'I regret, this is not known.'

'If harm came to him, it would mean war.'

'Precisely. Hence my rather dramatic warning about the Empire's future.'

A bewilderment such as I have never known settled upon me, and it seemed like a long time before I was able to raise my head from my hands. My friend had not moved.

'Holmes, what must we do?'

'Some things have been done already. I have arranged with Lestrade to be present at the meeting place before the Spanish Minister for Foreign Affairs arrives tomorrow. I trust you will accompany me?'

'As ever.'

A rare softness came into his eyes. 'My Watson never changes.'

I tried to assume his cold approach towards the task ahead, not very successfully. 'Tell me then Holmes, how things are to be.'

#

I took my watch from my waistcoat pocket and peered at it by the light of the moon. It was now four in the morning, and the first glimmer of dawn was a streak in the eastern sky. We had been here, in this closed police wagon, for more than an hour.

'You are sure, Mr Holmes, that they will come today?' In the darkness, Lestrade moved in his seat to relieve the cramp that was setting in.

From his position opposite me, I heard my friend reply. 'They will come. It would be a paramount act of foolishness to continue the risk they are running, when the substitution could be made today.'

'Thank God,' I said, 'that this plot was discovered, and that the Prime Minister will be far from here.'

'But, thanks to Mycroft, all indications are that he is already here to meet the Spanish Minister, when in fact the meeting has been reappointed and will take place elsewhere later today. My brother's influence has ensured that the newspapers were misleading on that point.'

'I have had their man who was watching Mr Abrahams arrested,' Lestrade said without taking his eyes from the gates. 'My men did not notice anyone else loitering nearby.'

'Barker is very proficient,' Holmes acknowledged. 'So, we are now dealing with the remaining three, led by Bekker.'

We fell silent and I looked ahead in the gathering light. The straight gravel path led from the guarded gates to the house, perhaps half a mile distant. Berrymount Manor was a two-storey structure in the Georgian style, wide with a round tower surmounted by a weather vane protruding from its midst. Holmes had mentioned that a red carpet and other temporary additions had been installed in advance to give the appearance of an impending foreign dignitary's visit.

'I think we should take up our positions now, Lestrade.' he said as he adjusted his ear-flapped cap.

At the inspector's order, the driver shook the reins and the horse moved slowly along the path, followed by the second wagon containing six armed constables. We had gone less than halfway to the house when we passed a group of trees on our left, while the ground fell away in a steep bank to our right.

'This will do,' Holmes decided.

We all got out and the wagons returned in the direction they had come, leaving the path eventually for concealment among four mighty oaks nearer the gates. Four constables hid themselves among the trees, while Holmes, Lestrade and I lay on our stomachs on the slope opposite with the remaining two.

It was a cold morning. On arrival I had noticed a faint mist around the base of the trees and a heavy dew upon the grass. We were in the heart of the Surrey countryside and our party was made up of two additional constables that Lestrade had requisitioned from the Dorking force to supplement the four from Scotland Yard.

Almost two hours passed.

'Look!' Lestrade said urgently, and we all turned to watch the gates.

A four-wheeler had arrived, and the guards at the gates conversed with the driver. After a few moments entry was allowed, and the gated closed heavily.

'At last,' Holmes whispered.

'How did they get past the sentries so easily?' I wondered aloud.

'This was all planned carefully in advance, Watson,' my friend replied. 'They would not have let such a small difficulty deter them, although I confess I do not yet know how it was overcome.'

The coach advanced at a slow trot until it had drawn near. From the trees across the path a constable emerged, waving his arms. The coach obediently came to a halt.

'Who goes there?' he demanded.

'We are a special auxiliary bodyguard for the Spanish Minister for Foreign Affairs,' came the reply tinged with foreign accent. 'Here to prepare for the arrival of His Excellency .'

The constable advanced, and I felt myself grow tense. He circled the coach and I was able to see four dark silhouettes within. Finally, he approached and asked for documentary proof, and was given papers which he examined and returned. He stepped back then, and peered into the coach.

'And who is the man accompanying you?'

'He is the chief assistant to His Excellency.'

'I think not, Herr Bekker.' Holmes said as we stood up beside Lestrade. 'I think not, indeed.'

From that moment, chaos reigned. The coach doors on both sides burst open and several shots were fired. A shotgun flared and the constable who had hailed the coach went down. The remaining constables, Holmes, Lestrade and myself returned their fire and the man with the shotgun sank to the ground. The huge figure of Bekker, dragging his prisoner with him in a clumsy stagger, ran for the trees firing as he fled.

Two constables fell to the remaining occupant, who fired from inside the coach. I emptied my service revolver into it and heard an agonised cry. A bullet whipped past Lestrade's face and he fired twice at Bekker in response.

'Careful, Lestrade, we must not hit the other man,' Holmes warned.

The little detective lowered his pistol as the fugitives disappeared into the trees.

I stumbled across the path with Holmes and Lestrade at my side. One of the fallen constables moaned in pain as we ran past, calling Lestrade's name.

'See to him. Lestrade,' Holmes shouted. 'They cannot escape now.'

Lestrade hesitated, and then stopped to attend his comrade. Holmes and I increased our efforts across the lawn, steadily gaining on Bekker. Garland Abrahams cried out as he was pulled mercilessly on. Bekker must have realised that we could not fail to overtake them, for he turned abruptly and they vanished behind a tall leafy hedge.

'It is a maze,' Holmes observed. 'If they have taken refuge there they are finished, since the only entrance is also the exit.'

‘One moment, Holmes.’ I paused to reload my pistol, and he did the same.

We approached the hedge cautiously, to find that it was indeed the beginning of a maze. Around the first corner we stopped, guns at the ready, but all that faced us was empty space. The only sound was a faint rustling from a breeze that had sprung up, and I was about to proceed when my friend gripped my coat sleeve.

‘Not that way, Watson. That pile of dead leaves over there is undisturbed, so they cannot have passed.’ He glanced around us. ‘On the other hand, I see that there is a fresh footprint in the mud at the end of this aisle. If this puzzle follows the traditional pattern I expect to find Herr Bekker and his unfortunate captive awaiting us at the end of the next row, for it will certainly be a dead end.’

Holmes was quickly proven correct. We rounded the corner with our backs pressed against the hedge to come face-to-face with Bekker, who held a pistol to his captive’s head.

‘Get back,’ he growled in his beard, and I noticed that his accent was thickened by fear. ‘Leave this place, and take all the police with you, or I will shoot this man.’

To my astonishment, Holmes lowered his revolver.

‘I am most surprised,’ he said in a mocking tone, ‘to find an agent of Imperial Germany hiding behind a helpless man. Have you no honour, sir?’

Bekker said nothing, but looked from Holmes to me and then back.

‘Has it occurred to you, Herr Bekker,’ Holmes continued, ‘that the moment you kill your prisoner you deprive yourself of your only protection against us?’

Bekker's expression remained unaltered, but I could sense that he was frantically searching his mind for a way out. Mr Abrahams was trembling uncontrollably, and was shaken in an attempt to make him still. 'I will do it, if you do not desist.'

'But what will you gain?' Holmes asked. 'If you destroy your shield we will cut you down, and you know this. If you surrender, and let him live, you will at least be alive until you face the hangman. You must see that this is the only choice you have. Come now, a man of your experience in your line of work should be able to tell when he is finished.'

I recall hearing my friend's voice fade away among the leafy walls surrounding us. Then there was a moment of absolute silence, I suppose while Bekker considered what had been said. I had the impression that Holmes knew something of this man, or of this type of man, that was lost to me, and a glance at his flint-like expression confirmed this.

Fear left Bekker's face, leaving it with a corpse-like blankness. Slowly, but very deliberately, he moved his pistol from his prisoner's head and placed it next to his own. With his eyes open he blew his brains out, and fell as his blood-spattered captive stumbled towards me.

'At least, this way he can be said to have died for his country,' Holmes said as we escorted Mr Abrahams, whose terror had turned to relief, away from the ghastly scene. 'I have no doubt that his death will be recorded like that.'

#

The constable that Lestrade had stayed behind to tend had died in his arms.

‘It should have been I who stayed while Lestrade accompanied you,’ I said as we left through the gates. ‘I could perhaps have saved his life.’

‘No,’ Holmes replied, ‘I saw the man’s wounds. They were mortal and your attention would have made little difference.’

‘I was able to ease the pain of the injured constables, at least.’

On our return to the scene, Lestrade had summoned the drivers of the police wagons who had been kept on hand as possible reinforcements, and dispatched one of them to bring medical help. I refused to leave until it arrived, and then the inspector had sent us back to Baker Street in the remaining wagon after having secured our promise that we would make a statement at Scotland Yard the following day.

As the grounds of Berrymount Manor receded, Holmes gave a long sigh.

‘Do not distress yourself, Watson. As always, you did all that you could.’

I earnestly hoped that he was right, and it gratified me that he thought so, but as our journey continued I found myself doubting and entering a melancholy state of mind. In effort to dispel this, I turned my thoughts back to the events of this morning.

‘You have explained much of this case, Holmes,’ I said at length, ‘but one thing still puzzles me.’

The wagon rattled over a cobbled street and he raised his head from his chest. ‘Just one?’

‘I mean about the intended substitution of Mr Garland Abrahams for the Prime Minister. How did they propose to effect this?’

'Sometimes I could believe that you are able to read my mind.' He gave a short laugh. 'I was in fact thinking of that very question. As I have already said, everything from beginning to end was meticulously planned, so we can be sure that their intentions were tried and tested. Perhaps Mycroft knows more, since he is much more acquainted with such people and their connections than you or I. Until I can speak to him we will have to be patient, but afterwards I will tell you what I can so that you can record this little affair as one of your over-dramatized stories.'

'They must have had some sort of help with their preparations, which means that there are more of their agents, or at least sympathisers, near at hand.'

'Undoubtedly.'

'So they are here, among us. Is there nothing we can do?'

'Nothing as yet, I am afraid to say, but when such ones show their hand we must be ready. For now, having left Mr Abrahams in Lestrade's charge and having ensured that his brother will shortly receive the good news, I can think of nothing but the luncheon that Mrs Hudson will shortly serve us.'

The Adventure of the Persecuted Accountant

During my long association with my friend and colleague Mr Sherlock Holmes there were numerous occasions when, at the insistence of my publishers, I found myself attempting to press him to relate or reflect upon those of our past adventures together that have been hitherto untold. Invariably he would decline to be forthcoming, so that I eventually realised that I had to watch for signs that a certain mood had overtaken him before I could expect any enlightenment as to his perspective on these incidents. And so there came an evening when he was between cases and I was desperate for new material, when I had approached the subject in various ways only to be always unsuccessful. Then, emerging from a long reverie as we sat smoking, he gave one of his quick smiles that told me that he had been aware of my objective throughout. Unexpectedly, he then narrated an account which I later prepared for publication as the story which follows…

Holmes sat opposite me, his mind elsewhere as our train came to rest at a country station. Our visit to Somerset had been a disappointment to him, he had quickly discovered the simple solution to a problem that had held such apparent intrigue at first sight. I joined him in looking out onto the tiny platform, where cloth-capped men stood with cages of racing pigeons and an occasional sheep as they waited for the slow local train to arrive. I noted, however, that my friend's attention was concentrated on the passengers who boarded and alighted, and those wandering, seemingly aimlessly, up and down before us. The smoke from our engine drifted by as a priest, his expression suitably solemn, appeared out of the cloud and passed along the platform.

"Such a misconception," Holmes mused.

"What have you seen, Holmes?"

He turned to me, emerging from a reverie.

"My apologies, Watson. I was following a train of thought."

"In what direction, old fellow?"

"I was absent-mindedly referring to the priest who walked along the platform, a moment ago."

"Doubtlessly, he is waiting for a later train."

"Without question."

Our train began to move slowly away, and the station was soon replaced by trees and fields of varying shades of green.

"Then what in particular interested you?" I asked him as our speed settled to a rhythmic pace.

"The emblem on the man's cassock."

I paused to bring to mind the scene of a few minutes earlier.

"To the best of my recollection it was black, except for a cross embroidered across the chest in gold thread."

"Precisely."

"Holmes, as to your reasoning I am all at sea."

From his expression, I saw that this was exactly the reply he had expected from me.

"I merely meant that the use of this symbol is quite wrong, although of course this would never be accepted because of long tradition."

"Do you then, deny the Crucifixion?" I queried in amazement.

"Not at all, only the use of the cross. Our Saviour was not put to death on such an implement."

It came to me that this was some sort of joke, for he had demonstrated an odd sense of humour often enough. On the other hand, he had at other times made pronouncements that I had initially dismissed, only for me to verify them privately later.

"I have read the description in the Gospels before now, Holmes. Kindly explain yourself."

"Gladly," He leaned towards me, speaking in more subdued tones. "You have read this in a modern translation of the Scriptures I am sure, often enough. But I am quoting from the original Greek writings, which is how the events were first recorded. The word used there for the object of impalement was stauros which, in the language of the time, is understood to mean a stake, or a tree. There is no way that it can be interpreted as a cross. Hence, I repeat, the importance given to the cross is a misconception."

"Then how did such an error come about? It seems unlikely, to say the least."

"Watson, the cross has been a religious symbol long before Christianity came into being. The version of it found on ancient Egyptian tombs is called an ankh. It was simply carried forward through other civilizations since, Greek, Roman and onward. Nor is this the only indication of my contention."

I drew myself up in my seat, to defeat the onset of cramp. "What else then, have you concluded?"

"You will recall that the account of the Crucifixion states that the Roman soldier in attendance drove a spear into the side of Our Saviour, on discovering that he had died."

"I believe you state it accurately."

“It then relates that blood and water, not just blood, mark you, gushed from the wound. The significance of this is that this could only occur if His arms were secured directly above His head, not at right-angles from His sides as they would have been with the use of a cross. As a medical man, you must agree.”

“I can hardly do otherwise, since your argument depends upon the spleen being ruptured. Holmes, you continually astound me with the depth of your knowledge.”

I was never to hear his reply, since the train was already losing speed and the outskirts of the capital had come into view. It came to rest and we alighted and were out of Paddington Station in moments. Within the hour, we were once more settled in our lodgings in Baker Street.

Luncheon was still two hours away but, hardly had we divested ourselves of our hats and coats, before our good housekeeper entered bearing the tea-tray. We sat at the breakfast table gratefully.

Presently, we attended to our accumulated post. Holmes, I think, had been hoping for a new case, but his grunts of dissatisfaction told me of his disappointment. He tossed aside several bills and an inconsequential letter or two, while I gave no more than a cursory glance to a medical journal and a reminder from a colleague of a forthcoming lecture on the subject of a smallpox outbreak in the north of England.

“Almost certainly introduced by foreign sailors from ships arriving at our ports.” He murmured.

“Holmes! How can you have known the contents of this paper?”

“There is no mystery, Watson,” he said in a bored voice. “The light from the window behind you is shining through the sheet as you hold it, and I recognise the letterhead. It is that of Doctor Trask who, as you have told me previously, serves as a self-appointed instrument to remind his colleagues of medical functions that he believes they should attend. There have been several articles in the papers over the past few weeks discussing new cases of smallpox, so it was a certainty that it would be at least part of the programme."

I was about to reply when I heard a coach pull up outside. I turned and saw from the window a young man paying off a hansom, before he strode purposefully towards our door.

"I do believe you have a new client, Holmes," I said as the door-bell rang.

A spark of interest appeared in his eyes and we listened in silence, as Mrs Hudson admitted our guest and they ascended the stairs. Moments later, she announced him as he stepped into the room.

"Mr Michael Burlott to see you, Mr Holmes."

We rose at once. "Mrs Hudson, pray bring another cup for our guest," he called as she left.

"No, not for me sir, thank you. I have not long had breakfast."

Holmes nodded and extended his hand. "I am Sherlock Holmes and this is my friend and colleague Doctor John Watson. If you would care to take the vacant armchair, we are at your disposal."

As Mr Burlott settled himself in front of the empty fireplace I studied him closely, as I knew Holmes would be doing also. Our visitor was above average height, though not excessively tall. His hair was of a light shade, and appeared quite unruly, while his skin was rather pale. His side-whiskers he had grown almost to his jawbone, and they framed a sombre face. I saw that his eyes were not clear but dull, and held little expression. He was dressed in a morning-suit of the style of several years ago, well-pressed but beginning to show signs of wear.

He was silent for a moment or two, I thought because he was unsure in the face of our expectancy, before blurting out the cause of his anxiety.

" Good sirs, I am here because I am being persecuted."

Holmes regarded him thoughtfully. "You have been openly threatened?"

"No, I received a note."

"Do you have it with you?"

Mr Burlott withdrew a crumpled sheet of paper from his pocket and handed it to Holmes. "I found it on the floor one morning, near my front door. There is no stamp, so it seems to have been delivered by hand."

"Quite so." Holmes produced his lens and scrutinized it. "The quality of the paper is poor and the ink also, since it leaves a watery impression. It bears one sentence, 'I know of your crime'. What does this refer to?"

"I have not the slightest notion."

"Surely, there is more to this. The letter is not a pleasant communication, but it is hardly persecution."

"There has been more, not letters but incidents, since I moved from Hammersmith."

Holmes looked at our client steadily. This was far from the first time that he had heard a story told in such a confused manner. Often, patience was needed from the beginning.

"Mr Burlott, I cannot help you if I do not have a clear understanding of your difficulty. Please take a moment to assemble your thoughts in their correct order, then relate them to us as they happened."

Our visitor inhaled deeply, and began in a quiet voice.

"My wife Sarah died, God bless her, two months ago. She was barely twenty years of age, and an orphan. We were married for less than six months."

Holmes and I murmured our condolences.

"I was left alone in our home in Hammersmith, with nothing but my work to distract me from my sorrows."

"May I ask, what is your work?" I enquired.

"His employment is of a clerical nature, Watson," Holmes retorted with an impatient glance in my direction. "Possibly an accountant."

Mr Burlott looked at him wide-eyed. "How did you discern that , sir? I have made no mention of it."

"By mere elementary observation. There is a faint ink stain on your right-hand shirt-cuff, and a red mark between your thumb and index finger where you hold a pen for prolonged periods. In addition, your trousers have become shiny from rubbing against the stool as you sit at your desk. What else am I to conclude, other than that your employment is in a shipping office or an accountancy establishment?"

"You are correct. I am an accountant, though still in training, at the firm of Ruthers, Settelworth and Fenner, on the Tottenham Court Road. It is a tedious life, but a living."

Holmes nodded. "But please continue with your narrative."

"Of course. This note arrived no more than two weeks after my wife's death, and caused me great distress for, as I have mentioned, I know not why this was sent to me nor who the sender might be. I dismissed it from my mind eventually, thinking it to be some sort of cruel prank, then I was almost run down by a landau one evening as I left my place of work. I knew then that my life was threatened."

"You are certain that the act was deliberate?"

"There is no doubt in my mind. The landau mounted the pavement at great speed, when there was no need. The road held only sparse traffic."

"This was on the Tottenham Court Road, you said?"

"It was."

"Did you confide your suspicions to the official police?"

"After some thought, I consulted Scotland Yard," Mr Burlott said, his face still expressionless. "I eventually secured an interview with Inspector Gregson, who I cannot say showed a great deal of interest. I felt that his impression was that I was making much from very little, but at my urging he stationed a constable outside my residence for a few nights."

"But more occurred after the officer was withdrawn," I suggested.

"Indeed. On two occasions since I have been followed by a hansom as I left my own conveyance on returning from my work in the evening. It is my practice to walk for part of the way. On shouting to challenge my pursuer the driver whipped up the horse and sped off, and once I was followed on foot. I stopped and stood to confront a man in dark clothing who immediately turned and retraced his steps, despite my calls to identify himself. It was after this that I decided to sell my house and move to Walthamstow."

"But that could not have been the end of the matter," Holmes observed, "or you would not be here today."

Mr Burlott raised his hands, then let them fall to his lap in a helpless gesture. "In truth sir, it was not the end. I settled into my new premises no more than a week ago, and no night has passed without some sort of continuance. Twice, during late evenings when a light ground mist sometimes appears, I have looked from my window to see a figure dressed in black and watching the house. I cannot imagine what his intentions are, but when I went out to confront him he had disappeared."

"This was the same man who followed you previously, and who drove the landau?"

"The very same."

"Can you describe him?"

"I was able to see him clearly only once, when he pursued me on foot. He is a fairly tall fellow, rather heavily-built and needs the attentions of a barber rather badly. More than that, I cannot say."

"You referred to more incidents," my friend recalled. "Pray relate them to us."

"One evening the top-hatted figure that he always was, appeared differently. Through the drifting mist I could see his shape, standing near the opposite side of the road. He appeared to float, no, to shimmer like a ghost or phantom, and in that moment my anger got the better of me. I keep a revolver, given to me by my late father from his military days, which I loaded before venturing into the street and firing at the man in an act of madness. I heard no cry or sounds of retreat, and I regretted my action later. However, when I examined the scene after the mist had cleared, which it had by the following morning, there was no sign that the incident had ever occurred!"

"No traces of blood, or impressions upon the ground indicating difficulty in walking or hurrying away?"

"None whatever."

"No marks, where your bullets had struck?"

"There are trees, spaced at intervals along the edge of the pavement. One of these bore gashes on its trunk."

"Have there been any more occurrences?"

"I believe," our visitor hesitated, but quickly continued, "that it was the evening following the events I have just described, when a bundle of tar-paper was pushed through my letter-box. It had been ignited and burned fiercely, but I was able to extinguish the blaze by pouring on a pitcher of water."

Holmes was silent for a short while, during which the only sounds were of coaches passing along Baker Street and the angry oaths which issued from the mouths of their drivers.

Finally, he fixed Mr Burlott with an enquiring look. "Describe to us now, if you will, your place of residence and its whereabouts."

"Well, Vine Street is a quiet place, to the extent that its residents are rarely seen out walking. I imagine most of them to be elderly and confined to their homes for most of the time. The villas are of dull brick and very nearly identical, with passageways between them leading to a parallel street. At the extremity of the road is the local Methodist church, so that a coach cannot leave in that direction, although the church can be reached from its far side." He paused, as if remembering something. "I should mention, gentlemen, that I shall not be at home tonight. I have a client in Colchester who I must visit on account of his infirmity, and I must say that I find the prospect of being away most agreeable."

"Understandably. Besides your employer and yourself, who knows of this?"

"No one else. I ensured that my superior would keep my intended absence to himself."

Holmes rose, and I did likewise. "A most advisable precaution. We can therefore be certain that these activities are likely to continue while you are away. I will be glad to look into this for you, Mr Burlott, and I suggest you leave me a key, to the back door if there is one, so that Watson and I can occupy your house in anticipation of a further assault until you return."

Our visitor seemed taken aback, but for no more than an instant. Clearly he had not expected such a suggestion, but he quickly recovered himself.

"But why…yes, I see the sense in that. I should explain that the premises have no back door but the rear entrance is situated instead at the side of the house, in the passageway that leads through to Calladine Street which runs parallel to Vine Street. My house is number 37."

"You will of course keep in mind," said Holmes as he pocketed the key, "that you must leave by this side entrance yourself, so that anyone watching from the front will be unaware of your departure, as they will be of our arrival later."

"I will remember."

"Excellent. All that remains then, is for you to state the hour when we are to call."

"I am to take the late afternoon train."

Holmes nodded. "Then we will be there shortly afterwards."

We could hear the clatter of pots and pans, as Mrs Hudson set about preparing luncheon. Mr Burlott took his leave and it fell to me to show him out. When I had done so I returned to our room to find that Holmes had draped his thin body across an armchair in what appeared to me as a most uncomfortable pose, and wore a slightly quizzical look.

"I should be interested to hear your impressions, Watson."

"Of the circumstances surrounding this affair?"

"No, of Mr Burlott."

I considered, for a moment or two. "He still suffers badly from the loss of his wife, I am certain. His face is almost devoid of expression, as his voice is of emotion. These are typical symptoms of severe shock or unsurmountable difficulty."

"I am sure that this is so," my friend replied, "and yet there is more to him, and to the story he told. I have identified six contradictions, the most obvious of which is the burning object pushed through his letter-box."

"I saw nothing suspicious, there."

"Not in itself, I agree. But would not the marks to the door and flooring be proof of his persecution that he could present to Gregson?"

"I suppose it would, but he said that Scotland Yard displayed little interest. Perhaps he was disillusioned with the official force."

"Yes, that must be why he sought our assistance." Looking thoughtful, he glanced at his pocket-watch. "But I see that the time for luncheon has arrived, and I hear our good housekeeper on the stairs. Let us fortify ourselves, before journeying to Walthamstow this afternoon."

#

We left the train at Wood Street Station, and quickly secured a hansom. Mrs Hudson had been quite surprised at Holmes' announcement that we were to spend another night away from our lodgings so soon, but that good lady made no comment and smiled resignedly, as usual.

"You seem certain, Holmes, that this enquiry will conclude after a single night," I remarked as the trees and fields gave way to the outskirts of a residential area.

"I have already drawn certain conclusions. If they are correct, then a stay for one night in Mr Burlott's house should suffice."

"Hence, our travelling-cases contain only toothbrushes and clean collars."

"Precisely. As for our sustenance, I recall that Mrs Braddock's Tea Shop proved adequate, when I had occasion to pursue a small matter here during my time in Montague Street. Since we passed it a few minutes ago, I know that it still functions."

At Holmes' direction, our driver reined in the horse, shortly after we passed the church that Mr Burlott had described. I saw a sign proclaiming a nearby thoroughfare to be Calladine Street and we alighted before a row of evenly-spaced villas.

“I imagine that we will find that this and Vine Street are very much alike,” my friend said as we watched the hansom pick up speed and disappear from our sight. “Now, Watson, let us find the passageway that will lead us to number 37. If the numbers in this street in any way correspond, we should not have far to go.”

In this he was quickly proven correct, for we had walked no more than a dozen yards before he turned abruptly.

“Is that the place, Holmes? The shadows make it difficult to see.”

“As we approach I think we will find that someone has been thoughtful enough to attach metal figures to the side door as well as, presumably, the front. Ah, I see that we have found the house we seek.”

He produced the key that Mr Burlott had given him, and we entered. I detected at once an atmosphere that lacked warmth. I attributed this to lack of female habitation, and wondered if my own lodgings from my bachelor and army days, or even those we lived in now, had a similar effect on strangers. We left our bags and wandered through the rooms. Again, a curious emptiness struck me. Holmes inspected every room, and remarked that one downstairs and two above were unoccupied and used, it seemed, only for storage. All that caught his attention was a scribbled note from Mr Burlott’s maid, acknowledging that she need not attend until further notice.

Back in the living-room, we removed our hats and coats.

“This room alone will serve our purpose,” he decided. “We have at our disposal a good-sized armchair and a chaise-longue. We will take turns at sleeping during the dark hours, for one of must stay on the watch at all times.” He went over to the large bay window and looked into the deserted street, not speaking. After some little time, I broke the silence.

"What do you see out there, Holmes, that interests you?"

"Exactly what I expected to see."

"And what is that, my dear fellow?"

"That the house opposite is empty. It is either derelict or for sale. That is where we must concentrate our attentions."

"But we have only just arrived. How could you have deduced that, already?"

"I have not. I knew it before we left Baker Street."

As many times before, he had quite confused me. "How is that possible?"

He turned to face me, the hint of a smile on his lips. "You will recall that Mr Burlott observed his tormentor to be tall and heavily-built."

"He did."

"And that, after the appearances in the mist, he disappeared without a sound?"

"I believe he said that, also."

"In other words, the man vanished. How can we explain that, other than concluding that he did not disappear or run away. A man of such stature would surely have made a noise."

"Do you mean that he was still nearby, but could not be seen?"

"That is exactly what I mean. I would wager that he hid behind that garden wall until Mr Burlott had ceased to search, and then simply re-entered the house."

I considered for a moment. "But did not our client also say that he fired on the figure, from close range?"

"Indeed, and there was no trace of injury afterwards. The explanation for that we have yet to discover."

We talked for a while more, then Holmes suggested that I leave the way we had entered for a visit to Mrs Braddock's Tea Shop. I enjoyed a good dinner there, and returned to Mr Burlott's house in the gathering dusk. Holmes had lit an oil lamp, ensuring that the place appeared to be occupied. He stared through a tiny gap in the curtains as I entered the living-room.

"The food was excellent, Holmes. I will take over now."

"There is no need. We will smoke for an hour, then if you wish you can sleep. I will continue with the first watch."

"My dear fellow, are you not hungry?"

"As you know, I have little appetite while on a case."

This was usual for him. I have known him go completely without sustenance for two or three days, saying that his active brain left no energy for digestion.

"Very well. Have you seen any signs of life, over there?"

"None. But the darker it gets, the more likely it is that something will occur."

It was, in fact, some time after midnight when the monotony was broken. I had just begun to take my turn when I fancied that there had been some movement in the front garden of the house opposite. I strained my eyes to see better, and saw it again. Among the blackness and the shadows of the trees cast by the rising moon, flames flared and grew.

"Holmes!" I called in hushed but urgent tones.

He was by my side instantly, never a deep sleeper.

"What have you seen?"

"A tall man in a top hat. I saw him as he set something afire."

"From the house across the road?"

"It appeared so. I think he is sheltering the flames beneath his cloak, to allow them to grow."

At that instant the figure became visible, illuminated by the fiery glow.

"He is about to make a second attempt to burn down this house," my friend observed.

We watched as the figure looked around carefully, to ensure that he was unobserved. I was about to remark that the precaution was probably unnecessary in a street and an hour such as this, when a commotion that I had been vaguely aware of grew noticeably louder. He stepped back, onto the pavement, as the noise grew louder still and a four-wheeler appeared, driven frantically with the coachman half-standing in his seat. In seconds the street was empty again, the coach now out of sight further along the thoroughfare and the figure nowhere to be seen.

"I fancy that there has been some sort of emergency, or circumstances of vital importance have arisen for our neighbours near the end of the road." Holmes said. "Unfortunately, our night visitor has been scared off."

"As you suggested earlier, Holmes, he must be living in that house opposite. Can we not approach him tomorrow, and tell him that we are aware of his intent?"

“I do not see that as a wise course, Watson, since he would doubtless deny any such purpose and we cannot prove otherwise, as yet. No, we must catch him in the act. Besides, I am certain that there is more to this.” He turned to me, and I fancied that I saw his eyes glint in the darkness. “Tomorrow I must leave you for a while. I intend to visit Somerset House briefly, and I anticipate that I will return much enlightened.”

We remained undisturbed for the rest of the night, though I slept little and resisted the temptation by sounds that were probably imagined to resume my vigil at the window. Holmes had insisted that I take the chaise-longue, and many were the times that I heard his movements and sensed his alertness in the nearby chair.

With the coming of morning we readied ourselves quickly, and my friend suggested that I visit Mrs Braddock’s establishment without delay, so that on my return he could set out. After a hearty breakfast I made my way back to Vine Street as soon as I could, to find him clad in his hat and coat and staring from the window as before.

“I shall find a hansom on or near Markhouse Road, Watson,” he said. “I cannot tell you at what time to expect my return. One thing it would be well to watch for is lights in the window of that house. You may see one, or perhaps two.”

“What will they be, Holmes?”

He half-turned as he made his way to the door. “Our friend over there will want to ascertain that Mr Burlott, as he believes, is still here, in preparation for another assault. To do this he will likely use a telescope or field-glasses. As the sun rises at the back of this house, you will see it reflected on whatever instrument he chooses to employ.”

“Which will also serve to assure us that he is still in residence,” I acknowledged.

"Precisely so."

He left without another word.

#

As always, Holmes was correct in his prediction. Just after mid-day, and again at three o'clock, two glowing orbs appeared briefly in the downstairs window of the house opposite. I watched from an angle of concealment, always careful to avoid touching the curtains and allowing our adversary a glimpse of my countenance. Occasionally, the silence and stillness of the street was disturbed by elderly residents taking the air, usually with the help of a stout stick, and by a trap delivering food. Once a hansom brought an upright gentleman who I deduced to be a doctor. I found coffee in Mr Burlott's kitchen and made myself a strong cup but food, I realised, would have to wait until Holmes' return.

This occurred in the late afternoon. He entered by the side door, so I did not see the conveyance that brought him, but he suddenly burst into the room in good spirits.

"I have discovered much, Watson," he began at once. "Also I visited Scotland Yard and Gregson will be arriving later."

"You anticipate that things will draw to a close tonight, then?"

"I shall be surprised if they turn out otherwise. However, the conclusion you may find unexpected."

He refused to be drawn further, but eventually encouraged me to leave the house for dinner after stating that he had ingested sufficient nourishment earlier. I found him, on my return, as I expected, staring as before from the window to the house across the street.

“We have some time before darkness, Watson. It will be as well to watch the house in case our adversary decides to vary his approach. At dusk we will light the lamps to signal to him that we are here, and then it is certain that he will respond.”

“Holmes, you have told me little of your activities of today.”

“All will become clear to you before this evening is out, old friend, never fear. One thing I must impress upon you, and that is that much about this affair has changed as a result of my discoveries. Therefore, when we confront this man, as we will later, you must on no account fire on him unless he shoots first, and then only to incapacitate him. If at all possible, we must capture him without injury.”

“By all accounts this man is a ruthless blackguard, Holmes, so I am bewildered by your instructions. I will of course comply, but the situation is beyond me.”

He smiled and took out his pipe. “But not for long, I assure you. Until then there is nothing to prevent us from enjoying our tobacco, as we wait for a further sign of his intent.”

And so we stood for hours, well away from any position that would have revealed us to outside view. As we talked of past cases and many other things, Holmes’ gaze never once moved from the house across the street, and the room grew cloudy with smoke.

Then dusk began to fall, and the failing light revealed to us that a lamp, turned well down, had been lit to illuminate the room that we watched. Holmes’ posture changed at once to that of a hunting dog after catching the scent, and I peered over his shoulder. Nothing more occurred until full darkness had fallen, and then the glow was suddenly extinguished.

“I think the last act is about to commence, Watson. If you would now leave by the side door passage and walk a little way down Calladine Street until you come to the next passageway, I would be obliged. Walk through until you emerge in Vine Street at a point further away, then cross the street and make your way back. When you reach the low wall that screens the front of the house we are observing, crouch behind it so that you cannot be seen as our friend approaches to conduct further acts of mischief. He is then cut off from his retreat, and I am here ready to confront him. He will not escape."

I put on my coat and hat. "I will go at once."

"Stout fellow."

More than ten minutes passed, by my estimation, before I took up an uncomfortable position as my friend had directed. A few feet ahead of me a coarse bush had become overgrown and hung over the wall above the pavement, and this added to my concealment. I drew my service revolver, but kept in mind Holmes' admonition that I should use it only if circumstances made it absolutely necessary. There was silence in Vine Street, except for the rustle of leaves and the far-off hooting of an owl.

I had just begun battling the onset of cramp, when I heard a door open softly. A cautious step drew nearer along the path, until the figure of a tall, heavily-built man with grey hair showing beneath his top hat, became visible to me in the dim light from a nearby lamp-post. He was still for a moment, until a coughing fit had passed, and it was then that I noticed that he carried a large stone.

He looked to the right and to the left, and then continued. As he approached the house where Holmes lay in wait he raised his arm above his head, but before he could hurl the stone the front door was flung open and my friend stood there with his pistol aimed.

“Good evening, Mr Enoch Dowling,” said he. “I would be much obliged if you would lay down your burden, as I have no desire to shoot you in my defence.”

Mr Dowling, for as such had Holmes referred to him, obeyed, and the stone fell to the ground with a dull sound. He did not surrender himself however, but turned in an attempt to run back whence he came.

I got to my feet and stepped into his path, my weapon held ready. “I will not fire unless you force me to,” I said as I beheld his surprised face. “Come now, we will go to join my friend together, and see how things are to be.”

Without a word he turned and preceded me, his breathing laboured. As he reached the house Holmes relieved him of the revolver he had kept in the pocket of his coat.

“I assume your intention was to throw the stone through the window and shoot whoever appeared at the door,” he ventured.

“There is no point in denying it,” Mr Dowling replied with great effort. “The time has come for me to rid the world of that scoundrel, Michael Burlott.”

“We are aware that you have conducted a campaign against him.”

Our prisoner raised his head, and I saw the ashen pallor of his face and knew at once that this man had not long to live. “I have indeed, gentlemen. I have sent him a note to make him aware that I know of his wickedness, and been a haunting cause of his troubles since. I hoped to drive him mad but my efforts seem to have had little effect, I had therefore decided to kill him tonight.”

“Why do you speak of Mr Burlott so?” I asked him. “What has the man done that offends you?”

"Offends me!" His voice rose, but his outrage was quickly cut short by a new bout of coughing. "He is the murderer of my sister. I expected to find him here tonight, but instead you gentlemen await me. Are you police, or has he hired you to kill me also?"

"We are not of the official force," Holmes explained, "although I have arranged for an inspector to arrive later. I am a consulting detective. My name is Sherlock Holmes, and this is my associate, Doctor John Watson. Mr Burlott availed himself of my services because of your pursuit."

"Ha! He is artful that one. I have no doubt that his true intent was to dispose of me also as soon as you informed him of my identity and whereabouts."

Holmes took him by the arm and guided him to a chair. "But I see that you are unwell. Sit there and Doctor Watson will pour you a glass of this fine brandy that Mr Burlott keeps, while I tell you of my own discoveries regarding your situation."

Breathing heavily, Mr Dowling obeyed and took the drink in one swallow. After a while he seemed calmer and Holmes enlightened us both.

"This morning I visited Somerset House and read something of your family records. I saw at once that your sister was not an orphan as she had told her husband, but had an older brother. Later I made other enquiries that revealed that you had rented the house opposite to that of Mr Burlott, and from there I went to Scotland Yard to inform them that I had investigated this matter and would conclude it this evening."

"You were very sure of yourself, sir."

"I have had much experience. Will you now relate to us the events that led up to your persecution of Mr Burlott?"

Mr Dowling waited while his heaving chest subsided. “Persecution? Yes it was that, and never was it more deserved. I worked in a bank, you see, in a position of trust, and made the greatest mistake of my life when I took money to pay my gambling debts. Embezzlement is a serious crime and I have paid for it, even though they let me free early due to the consumption I caught while in prison. I swear, had I been a free man, none of this would have occurred. I would have moved Heaven and Earth to have prevented the marriage of Michael Burlott to my dear Sarah.”

“What then, was your objection at the time?”

He hesitated and looked up at me. I refilled his glass and he drank before continuing. “Sarah came to see me, while I was in the cells. She told me of the man who was her intended and I warned her at once, for I knew him. Michael Burlott believes himself to be distantly related to the aristocracy and is determined to live as if that were recognised. He is obsessed with this notion and spends as if he were a lord. Money runs through his fingers like water. Sarah, of course, would believe nothing of his extravagances, and I understand that she kept up the pretence of being orphaned because she was ashamed that her only relative was a criminal. Burlott had represented himself to her as a rich and considerate man.”

“But why did he marry your sister, knowing that she had little money?” I enquired. “To do that, he surely must have loved her.”

“There was no love there, on his part, but greed drove him to ruin Sarah with a cruel plan.”

“How did this come about?”

Mr Dowling fought hard to suppress more difficulties with his breathing, then his shoulders slumped and he resumes his narrative.

"When I left prison I tried to find Sarah. She and Burlott had married by this time and he had taken her from her former home. I managed to discover the whereabouts of a friend of hers, a woman she had known for years and who she trusted like a sister, and to convince her that I was Sarah's brother. She told me that Sarah was the beneficiary of a legacy from a man she had tended in his old age, who had recently died. Sarah had sought to keep this from her husband for she had already discovered the truth of my warning, but he had somehow realised her good fortune. I knew that he would not rest until he had taken every penny from her."

"Was it to prevent him from harming her, that set you upon his track?" asked Holmes.

"Not at first. After some enquiries I discovered where Burlott lived and followed him, at first without his knowledge. This was not difficult, for he was too consumed with his own wellbeing and his obsession to pay much attention to most other things. One evening I was close behind when he visited a tavern, and met a crowd of ruffians who he proceeded to drink heavily with. As the hours wore on they became very drunk and he began to tell them the intimate details of his life with Sarah. Listening to the indignities he heaped upon her, my anger grew so strong that I could barely control myself. I was on the point of getting to my feet and accosting him openly, of thrashing him thoroughly, when he began to relate the worst of his intentions."

"Those that led to her death. I presume?"

"Exactly that, Mr Holmes. He boasted of his cleverness in introducing opium to my Sarah, without her realising what she was taking. He represented the drug to her as a cure for the persistent backache that had plagued her for some months. Of course she deteriorated quickly, her behaviour becoming more and more outrageous and unstable, and Burlott lost no time in committing her to an insane asylum. On hearing this, my fury dissolved into grief. You will understand, gentlemen, how I was aware of nothing but the pain as I left that place. After a while the shock began to fade and I resolved to visit the place to see my sister. If I was torn before, imagine my agony when I was told that she had passed away in a dark cell with the screams of lunatics ringing in her ears."

I could not help but feel sorry for the man.

"It seems to me," I said to Holmes, "that this man has committed no crime, except for his attempts to set this house afire."

"And his intention to murder Mr Burlott this evening. However, if this account is genuine I am not without sympathy and we will be guarded in our revelations to Gregson. I will recommend to him that he urges the court to deal with Mr Dowling with leniency." He turned to our prisoner, who was now sitting with his head in his hands. "One thing still puzzles me, Mr Dowling. I recall from our conversation with Mr Burlott that he faced a dark figure at which he discharged his pistol, near the house across the street. He stated that it disappeared without trace. Can you furnish an explanation for this?"

For the first time, a ghost of a smile crossed the ailing man's features.

"Yes sir, that is easily explained. My intention, as I have mentioned, was to drive Burlott mad with my appearances, until his behaviour caused him to be committed as he had done to my Sarah. Seeing that this was proving ineffective, I decided to add to his troubles by seeming to be unaffected by his retaliations. I found a piece of black cloth among the sparse contents of the house and cut out a figure that was roughly the shape of a man. I hung it from the bushes over there, where the glow from the street-lamp would barely illuminate it. I believe that luck was with me that night, for it was then that Burlott chose to use his weapon, as you say. That cloth is in the house still, with bullet holes in it that would have been in me, otherwise."

Holmes pondered for a moment. "That quite settles it. As far as you know, did Mr Burlott succeed in obtaining your sister's legacy?"

"I understand that some complications arose. There was a clause in the Will that forbade the award reverting to a third party, even a spouse."

"Our Mr Burlott was not very thorough, if he did not anticipate that. Desperate men often overlook vital details." He was silent abruptly, and sat listening. "Ah, I believe I hear Gregson's police wagon approaching. I do hope he has the presence of mind to tell the driver to take it further down the street, where it cannot be seen from here."

#

Gregson had been with us fully two hours, before we heard a hansom discharge its passenger in Vine Street, near the front door of number 37. Moments later, Mr Michael Burlott burst into the room and dropped his overnight case to the floor.

"Mr Holmes, Doctor Watson…." He fell silent as he caught sight of Mr Dowling. "Is this the scoundrel who has been haunting me? You have done well, gentlemen, to rid me of him. I must send a telegram to Scotland Yard."

Gregson moved into the pool of light cast by the oil-lamps. "That is quite unnecessary. The force is already represented here. All is known, Mr Burlott."

"We have heard the truth of it," Holmes confirmed.

Burlott stood stock-still. His eyes took on a different look and swept from one face to another, as if seeking one who would defend him. Then panic filled his face and he turned and ran from the room. As we heard his hurried steps recede I realised that no one in the room had moved. I rose to look from the window and saw a burly constable lead our client away in handcuffs.

"I took the precaution of stationing an officer at both front and rear doors," Gregson said then, "with orders to immediately arrest any man trying to flee. Of course, until I heard your explanation, Mr Holmes, I had thought that this would be Mr Dowling, but fortunately we now have the right man."

"You will remember, Gregson, how I have shed light on his part in this?"

"I will, and I will do what I can in his favour."

"Then," said my friend, "there is nothing more that needs to be done to conclude this affair, save perhaps pouring a glass of Mr Burlott's excellent brandy for each of us before we go our separate ways."

The Adventure of the Second Whitechapel Murderer

It was an unseasonably fine day at the beginning of the Spring of 1895 when, returning to our Baker Street lodgings after an invigorating morning walk, my friend Mr Sherlock Holmes and I had hardly closed our front door when a harsh rapping upon it surprised us. We glanced at each other and he turned back at once and opened the door wide.

"Lestrade, my dear fellow," he cried with some astonishment. "What has brought you to us in such an excited state? I think it would be as well if you came in and took coffee with us, so that you can explain when you have recovered your composure."

The little detective mumbled his thanks and took the stairs with us, and Holmes called to Mrs Hudson before we entered our sitting room.

When we had settled ourselves my friend looked at the inspector with some curiosity, as we awaited the arrival of our coffee.

"I cannot recall seeing you in such an agitated frame of mind previously, Inspector. What can have transpired to induce this?"

Lestrade's bulldog-like countenance took on a look that I interpreted as near to despair. "Mr Holmes, I thought we had finished with this dreadful business, though we were unable to get anywhere with it."

At that moment our good housekeeper entered with a tray of cups and a steaming coffee-pot, and so silence prevailed until she had left. I rose then and began to pour, as Holmes replied.

"To what do you refer, Lestrade?"

"The Whitechapel murders, of a few years ago. As far as we know at the Yard, Mary Kelly was the final victim. There has been none other since November of 1888."

Holmes nodded, as I handed both men their cups. "She was, as you say, the last known to be slain, although I am far from certain that we are aware even now of all the victims in that case. There were several other women of the streets murdered, during the reign of terror." He frowned. "But I understood that Scotland Yard had all but given up the investigation after so long, so why are you concerning yourself with it now?"

The inspector drank and put down his cup. "The Yard never closes a file until the culprit is behind bars, Mr Holmes. What I am upset about is the new murder of last night."

My friend and I exchanged glances of unpleasant surprise, our coffee forgotten as we stared at Lestrade.

Holmes spoke first. "Was the body dismembered in the same fashion? Are there identical features to the crime?"

The Inspector took out his notebook, turned to a page and read from it. "Lottie Burrows, aged about twenty-six. Found by a constable around midnight while on his beat in Whitechapel. She was lying in an alley with an immense gash, thought to be from a surgeon's knife, carved from her chest down to her stomach. Does that not sound familiar, Mr Holmes?"

Holmes' frown deepened. "There are certain characteristics in common with the previously known victims, such as the location of the murder and the fact that a scalpel was considered to be the murder weapon. This woman was a lady of the night, I presume?"

“You put it so delicately, Mr Holmes, but of course you are right. What other sort of woman would be in such a place at that time?”

“Quite so. I should however remind you, Lestrade, that my intended investigation at the beginning of the original murders was halted by Scotland Yard. I endured the chastisement of yourself, Gregson and Hopkins simultaneously in this very room, as I recall.”

The inspector looked away, fixing his stare on the carpet for a few moments. “To this day, I swear I know not why we were ordered to come here and speak to you in such strong terms. I can only suspect that Commissioner Sir Charles Warren wanted only Edmund Reid and Abberline on the case.” He hesitated, before adding. “I suspect that something you said was reported in the press and reached the wrong ears.”

Holmes shrugged. “It was certainly featured in an article in The Standard, quite erroneously, that I had hinted at the involvement of royalty or freemasonry, at the fringes of this affair. I suppose that suggestion would have been enough to exclude me from all further proceedings, if it were taken seriously in certain quarters. I do think, however, that a little discussion between us could have cleared this up, had you sought an explanation before acting on the strength of the assumptions of an over-enthusiastic young reporter.”

“I can assure you that we were following orders, Mr Holmes. It did not sit well with either my colleagues or myself.”

“And so,” Holmes smiled suddenly, leaning forward in his chair and clapping his hands, “we reach our present situation, which may or may not be connected. Tell me then, Lestrade, how do your superiors view this new outrage?”

There was a moment of silence in the room, when the only sound was from the passing hansoms and four-wheelers in Baker Street.

"When I suggested any connection to the previous murders, it was ignored, I know not why. It was as if I had never spoken. Someone is hiding something, I am sure. Perhaps after all, there is truth in that newspaper article."

"At any rate," my friend said then, "it can do no harm to look into this since Scotland Yard appear to consider it a separate enquiry, as it may yet be. But, as you say, it cannot completely be ruled out that the original Whitechapel murderer may be responsible. I feel that it would be churlish to turn my back on the situation, despite the Yard's previous attitude to me regarding the matter. If you are confident, Inspector, that you will not be subjected to the wrath of your superiors for involving Doctor Watson and myself, we will glad to accompany you to the mortuary where I will make my own examination of the body of this unfortunate woman."

#

We travelled together in the four-wheeler that Lestrade had waiting. This was not the first time I had visited the Whitechapel Workhouse Mortuary, where the body of Lottie Burrows had been taken, and I was anticipating without pleasure renewing my acquaintance with the place. It was situated in a large yard off Old Montague Street, a small brick building that I would have described as little more than a shed. We entered through the gates at the end of a narrow alley known as Eagle Place, and from Holmes' expression I gathered that he had not seen the place before.

The windows were of insufficient size to admit much natural light, but a number of oil lamps aided visibility. A man wearing a stained leather apron over his morning suit emerged from the surrounding shadows and extended his hand to the inspector with a pleasantness that surprised me, for it is far more usual for those with such an occupation to be of a disposition that reflects it. Lestrade introduced him as "Doctor Phillips, the appointed Police Surgeon to H Division."

"I take it that you wish to examine the body of the woman Lottie Burrows, Doctor Watson?"

"Not I, but my friend."

Doctor Phillips regarded Holmes curiously. "Did you not state your profession as consulting detective, sir?"

"Indeed so. Be assured that I have acquired sufficient knowledge to conduct such an inspection."

The mortuary doctor glanced at Lestrade, who nodded.

"Very well. I will be nearby, if you need me."

"I would be grateful," Holmes said, "if you would remain."

"As you wish."

At that, Holmes proceeded to walk slowly around the table we had been led to, his eyes half-closed in concentration as he mumbled to himself. He stopped suddenly and leaned closer to the body.

"Doctor Phillips, have you made further incisions during your examination?"

"I have not yet made my examination. I was preparing to do so when you arrived."

“Then this long gash, from the trachea almost to the abdominal area, was sustained during the attack?”

“Presumably. As I said, I have done little as yet, apart from conduct some preliminary observations.”

“Did they reveal to you that the heart has been removed?”

I heard a sharp inhalation from Lestrade, and concealed my own surprise.

“Indeed they did. I was about to remark upon it.”

Holmes looked up from the body. “Did anything else strike you?”

“I trust you are referring to the incision itself. This was carried out with considerable surgical skill. If there is one thing I can tell you with confidence, gentlemen, it is that whoever did this was no crude butcher.”

Holmes nodded slowly. “My thanks to you, Doctor. Your information has been of immense assistance.” He turned towards us. “I think there is little more to be learned here. Come gentlemen, we can now leave the good doctor to his work.”

#

Outside, we crossed the yard and stood before the coach.

“Lestrade, have the newspapers any knowledge of this, any at all?”

The inspector shook his head. “No, Mr Holmes. As I said earlier, my superiors wish to avoid any association of this with the other murders. The incident will be treated as a separate, unconnected crime. Also, a disclosure to the contrary would almost certainly cause panic.”

"Quite. It is of paramount importance that no specific details are released of the things we have just learned, nor of the crime itself."

"I have already taken such steps, although the newspapers seem to have their own sources of information sometimes, as we know. For my part, the constable who found the body and all others involved since have been sworn to silence as to all but the most basic information."

"Excellent. While this is maintained, we have a good chance of early success."

Lestrade's expression lightened. "It appears as if I was right after all, don't you think, about the connection to the original Whitechapel killings? I'm sure we all remember that the murderer, although he was never found, was perceived to possess such skill as we have just heard Doctor Phillips state was used upon Lottie Burrows."

"That is still possible, although the removal of the heart alone suggests other motives, perhaps a different killer."

"There is little more to be done," said the inspector, "until I receive Doctor Phillips' report at the Yard. I expect it later today."

"One line of enquiry is open to us at once." Holmes disagreed. "You will recall that, before my 'interference' was forbidden by the Yard, I suggested that some effort should be made to establish whether the previous victims were known to each other. As far as I am aware, this was ignored. Perhaps now, Lestrade, you might care to ascertain if there is any connection between these women and our present subject, Lottie Burrows."

"I will most certainly look into that, on my return to the Yard."

“God forbid that there should be further victims,” I interjected.

I caught a quick glance from Holmes. “Indeed, Watson. And now, Inspector, I am sure that you will want to continue your enquiries from Scotland Yard. No, our thanks to you, but Watson and I will walk for a while rather than share your conveyance again. I find that exercise often promotes constructive thought.”

#

Holmes said little as we walked. Several times I made to speak, only to be dissuaded by his expression and the knowledge gained from experience: when he is deep in thought in the midst of a case, he is best left alone.

Eventually we came upon a hansom that had just delivered its fare, and so made our way back to Baker Street. I can recollect him making but one remark, during the journey.

“There are similarities, Watson, yes. And yet, from a few years ago, there is something…..”

This new case was clearly playing upon his mind, haunting him. It did not surprise me therefore that he instructed Mrs Hudson on our return that he would not be requiring luncheon, and scoured his index as I ate.

“That was a delicious kedgeree, Holmes. You really should eat.”

“I have no time, or energy to spare. If my hypothesis is in any way correct, then there is much to do. However, old fellow, I would be obliged if you would ask our good lady to bring a pot of strong coffee.”

This I did, and as we drank together I asked if he had made progress.

"Some, I believe, although I am far from certain. If I am right I fear that more blood will be spilled soon. Tell me, Watson, are you of the opinion that, for example, a man's severed arm or leg, could somehow be reattached to his body to function as before?"

I smiled. "Holmes, this is quite impossible, although I believe it has been attempted many times before now. During my service in Afghanistan I heard old legends of successes by mythical miracle-makers, but nothing as regards truth. No, I regret that medicine cannot achieve such things, and may never."

He nodded slowly. "As I thought, and yet…"

Neither of us felt an inclination to leave our rooms that afternoon, as the first signs of a dense fog were already apparent in the street below. Holmes returned to his index while I read the mid-day edition of The Standard, but gave up after a short while. As we sat in our armchairs and smoked he would not be drawn as to his discoveries, as was his custom until he was quite certain that his case was complete. Mrs Hudson served us with an excellent steak and kidney pie that was more than sufficient for us both, but Holmes merely toyed with his before pushing away his plate.

As I rose from the table, I chanced to glance out of the window.

"Holmes, we are about to receive a further visit from Inspector Lestrade."

He closed his eyes for a moment. "I have feared this, since we left him earlier."

We heard Mrs Hudson on the stairs, and then Lestrade burst into the room. "Gentlemen, good evening. I fear I have some terrible news."

"Who is the latest victim, Lestrade?"

"Mr Holmes, how could you have known? I have come straight from…"

"I expected it," my friend replied gloomily. "It was highly probable if my theory is correct, and yet I could do nothing to prevent it. Pray tell me what has happened, and of any similarities or common factors shared by the killing of Lottie Burrows."

The inspector sat at Holmes' bidding, but refused a cigar or glass of porter.

"A young woman, younger than the first, met the same fate in Whitechapel, less than an hour ago. Her name was Jane Moulder."

"Was her heart removed, also?" I enquired.

"It appears so, Doctor. The physician who was present saw this immediately, and I expect confirmation from Doctor Phillips, before long."

"She was a lady of the night, as before?" Holmes asked.

"She was, starting her trade early this evening. Her killer must have been watching for her, no doubt using this accursed fog as concealment. We can hardly dismiss the evidence now – this is the Whitechapel Murderer again."

Holmes shook his head, slowly. "No, I cannot see that as most likely, despite the similarities to the killings before. Lestrade, have you given any thought to my suggestion of making comparisons with Lottie Burrows?"

"I saw from my notes, as soon as I added the entries for this evening," the inspector produced his notebook and turned over several pages, "that there are two things shared by both women."

"Enlighten us, pray."

"Both worked regularly out of the same tavern. That is the White Hart, at 89, Whitechapel High Street."

"I recall that place from the previous murders, Holmes," I remarked.

"Quite so, Watson," he agreed.

"Again, it points to the same murderer," Lestrade insisted.

Holmes leaned back in his chair. "We shall see. What of the second feature that the women had in common?"

"They both attended, from time to time, the free clinic in Brick Lane, not far away. I understand that it is run by Doctor Lawson Venables, the Harley Street surgeon, as a charitable enterprise."

"Excellent, Inspector." Holmes expression lightened at once. "Well, unless you have anything else to tell us, I see that you are anxious to return to the Yard. I will, I assure you, keep in mind the most revealing similarities between these murders and the previous Whitechapel case that you have so astutely recognised. I am quite certain that we both will know more soon."

With that Lestrade was dismissed, looking rather bemused. Myself, I experienced no surprise when my friend turned to me as the inspector descended the stairs.

"Watson, what do you say to an evening enjoying the company of the revellers in the White Hart Tavern, in Whitechapel High Street?"

"I cannot say I relish the notion."

"Am I then, to pursue this alone?"

"You know me too well, Holmes."

"I was certain of it. Come, old fellow, let us retrieve our hats and coats and see if we can find a hansom in this thickening fog."

#

It proved difficult, but after a short walk we came upon a conveyance waiting nearby. The fog swirled about us and horse trod carefully, no doubt confused by the limited visibility, but we eventually arrived in a narrow and dismal street.

"I presume the tavern to be in that direction," Holmes said as the surrounding fog muffled the cab's retreat, "since it is there that the only lighted window is visible."

We walked across to the opposite pavement, twice narrowly missing figures that loomed suddenly before us. As we neared the tavern much raucous laughter and the sound of a singing voice strained to its limit reached our ears, as did the succession of jumbled notes of an attempted accompaniment on a badly-tuned piano.

Through the shifting haze I saw that a series of arches bridged the badly-lit street as it continued on past the tavern. From that direction I heard the cries of women who had lost their companions or who were plying their trade with difficulty. The drumming of horses' hooves came to us and immediately ceased. We entered into an uproar of sound and confusion, as the 'entertainment' continued and customers jostled each other, not always good-naturedly, near and around the bar. I found the thick smoke-laden atmosphere oppressive, but was relieved to see that our appearance attracted no particular attention. I would have expected some initial scrutiny in a place unaccustomed to the patronage of gentlemen, but then I saw several fellows in evening clothes, one a local member of parliament, drinking heavily with (I assumed) local young women precariously balanced on their knees. I now knew the answer to an unspoken question: why had Holmes not employed disguises for this venture?

My friend caught the eye of a young man, hardly more than a child, who served as a waiter. Shortly afterwards we were sitting at a corner table with two pints of ale before us. The glasses were smudged, and neither of us drank.

For the next two hours or so we were engaged in an activity that I found acutely embarrassing, and so will not record in detail here. Suffice it to say that Holmes and I were approached, as he intended, by several women who worked in the tavern or from it. He was his most charming self, buying drinks and subtly introducing questions into the conversation. When he was satisfied and we were again alone at our table with our drinks untouched, he leaned towards me and spoke softly.

"There is nothing more to be learned here, Watson. Most of these women knew both Lottie Burrows and Jane Moulder, but can provide no useful information as to who might have had reason to wish them harm or bring about their deaths."

"A wasted evening then, and not one I would care to repeat."

He laughed quickly. "I must apologise for causing you such discomfort, old fellow, but our time may not have been so uselessly spent as you imagine."

"But you, yourself, said that we had learned little."

"True, but for the last hour or more I have been observing that fellow leaning against the bar. From both his and the barman's demeanour it seems obvious that they are strangers to each other, and he is therefore unlikely to be found here regularly. What do you conclude then, when I tell you that since his arrival, which was not long after ours, he has been ensuring constantly that we have not moved from our seats? I imagine that his field of vision must be exceptionally wide, since he has hardly found it necessary to turn his head."

Through the heavy veil of smoke I saw that he referred to a short, sallow-faced man, wearing a black bowler.

"You believe he has followed us here?"

"I am certain of it."

"In the fog?"

"That explains why I was unaware of it."

"Do you know him, Holmes?"

My friend gave an almost imperceptible nod. "I do, of old. His name is Saul Naughton, a paid assassin by trade. He was certainly behind the disappearance of two witnesses in the Aquinas-Piper scandal. His involvement was never proven, but the case was dismissed. Had it been placed in my hands, the embezzlers would now be in Dartmoor and Naughton would have gone to the gallows."

Keeping my gaze away from the man, I asked: "But why is he pursuing us? Could he be the murderer of those two women?"

"That is of course possible, as things stand now, but unlikely since he works strictly for payment. As to how it came to be, I surmise that this new Whitechapel killer returned to the scene of one or other of his crimes and saw Lestrade there. Possibly out of curiosity he then followed him to Baker Street and realised that we were conducting a parallel investigation. Seeing us as a threat to his purpose, whatever it may be, and not being skilled in any other form of murder but that which he has demonstrated, he hired a professional. Hence the presence of Naughton here tonight. There are, of course, other possible explanations, but that is the one that immediately suggests itself."

"If he is as competent as you imply, we are in great danger, Holmes."

"But not for the first time. Do you have your service revolver with you?"

"My hand rests upon it in my pocket."

"Capital. I also am armed. "We will, I think, make it difficult for our professional murderer to earn his pay."

He rose, and I did likewise. "It may take some searching to find a cab on a night such as this," he said more loudly, "so it would be as well to be on our way."

As we neared the door I noticed that Mr Saul Naughton avoided looking in our direction. Once outside, and I felt at once relieved to be free of the clamour in that place, Holmes took my arm and guided me to the shadows of a deep doorway across the street. A few moments passed before Naughton emerged, peering into the fog in both directions before setting off the way we had arrived. As the fog swirled around him and finally engulfed him, we stepped from concealment and my friend's voice sounded strange in the dull silence.

"We will see more of him soon, I think. This way, Watson."

He led us along the side of the tavern, to where the street continued with periodic arched sections above and shiny cobbles underfoot. Lamps shed a meagre glow at intervals, penetrating the fog hardly at all, and Holmes paused to listen often.

"Why have we chosen this way, Holmes?"

"To make it easier for our friend, Naughton. As soon as he concludes that he is no longer on our track he will hurry along here to overtake us. Doubtlessly, he is thinking that the fog will aid in his concealment and that of his intended crime."

We stood very still, the silence and the heavy fog surrounding us.

"I hear nothing."

"Nor I, as yet. Patience, Watson."

We walked on, groping with the uncertainty of the blind and continuing to listen after every few yards. Once a cat ran out of the gloom, startling me, and the dripping of escaping water from an unseen source sounded loud because of the insulating properties of the fog, but we saw no sign of human habitation. Then Holmes listened again, for longer.

"I was right. We are being followed."

"I heard no footsteps."

I stood close enough to see him shake his head. "It is a coach that pursues us, at a frantic speed."

"How can you be sure that it is Naughton?"

"I cannot, and if it is some other nothing amiss will occur as he passes us by. However, I cannot imagine many of the residents hereabouts leaving their homes on a night such as this, so keep your weapon ready."

At that we kept to the narrow pavement, moving close against a whitewashed wall. I could now hear the drumming of horses' hooves on the cobblestones, getting louder with the passing of every instant. We waited.

Even with the muffling effect of the fog, the sound became deafening, before a brougham pulled by four black stallions burst into view beneath an arch a few yards behind us. In a moment of clarity I recognised the silhouette of a man in a bowler hat whipping up the horses and cursing continuously, before Holmes gripped my arm and shouted into my ear.

"Run!"

We took to our heels at once, the echoes of our footfalls like dull hammer-blows upon the cobbles. The street was too narrow for the coach to pass without striking us and my friend had seen this and sought to shelter us. The brougham was gaining on us with great speed and I was sure that the next moment would bring death to us both, for the doorways that presented themselves were far too shallow for our purpose. I could feel the horses' breath (perhaps only in my imagination) and the crack of the whip seemed near to my face while the hooves threatened to trample me to the ground, but Holmes gripped my arm once more and pushed me against two dilapidated gates that were loose enough on their hinges to allow us space.

The coach thundered on and I caught a glimpse of the driver looking back over his shoulder and pointing something towards us across an upraised arm.

"Down, Watson."

We sank to the ground as a dull explosion erupted like cannon fire. I recognised the sound as a shotgun blast as we got to our feet and discharged our revolvers several times. We were rewarded with a cry of pain, as the fog closed around the brougham. The sound of hurrying hooves faded, and silence descended once more.

"After our small excitement, I think we should retrace our steps and attempt to procure a conveyance." Holmes said as he brushed dust from his coat.

Doing likewise, I glanced at the scarred and torn remains of the gate. The shotgun blast had all but shredded much of the wood . We made our way back to the tavern with some difficulty, to discover a scuffle taking place outside. We emerged from the fog to see two men, accompanied by ladies of doubtful repute, hammering away at each other while the innkeeper and other customers cheered them on. It became apparent that the cab standing nearby was the source of the disagreement, each party claiming it as his own because of the unlikelihood of finding another in this inclement weather.

An impatient cabby shouted down at the combatants as he gripped the reins impatiently. "Come on now, gentlemen. Hurry and settle this, will you? I could have taken half a dozen fares, while I'm waiting here on a night like this."

We were on our way in an instant, Holmes having offered the fellow double the fare if he took us at once. He said little during the journey, the attempt on our lives appearing to cause him no dismay. It was I who spoke first, when we were once again safely in our rooms.

"Are you all right, Holmes?"

"Perfectly."

"You are not perturbed by our experiences tonight?"

He smiled faintly. "Not at all. I foresaw something of the like at the appearance of Naughton."

"Is he dead, do you suppose?"

“I have no way of knowing. Doubtless we will learn more when we relate our evening’s work to Lestrade, tomorrow morning. For now, Watson, I will wish you goodnight.”

As the door of his room closed behind him, I wondered what it was that he had seen or remembered about these hideous crimes that had escaped me unnoticed. Was it, as Lestrade continually suggested, some common feature with the original murders, or some other similarity known only to him? The question haunted me as I lay searching for sleep, until it finally overcame me.

#

“Hurry, Watson, I can recommend the kippers.” My friend seemed in unexpectedly good spirits as I emerged from my room. His own breakfast plate was a scene of devastation, and he had already called for and received a second pot of coffee.

“You indicate that time is short, Holmes. We have a full day ahead, then?”

“Indeed. You will recall that I mentioned that we must visit Scotland Yard first thing. After that, I think we will make the acquaintance of Doctor Lawson Venables.”

I took my place at the table, and Holmes rang the bell.

“As the physician serving both victims,” I said, “perhaps he will throw some light on the matter.”

“I have no doubt that he will furnish us with some most valuable information,” Holmes replied as my breakfast was set before me, “whether is he aware of it or not.”

#

The fog of last night had cleared completely. Mid-morning had arrived by the time we found ourselves seated in the familiar confines of Inspector Lestrade's office. We had been kept waiting, unavoidably, while he issued instructions to the latest shift of constables responsible for the Whitechapel area. Holmes had once mentioned that their beats were set out in such a way as to overlap every fifteen minutes. I hoped that local residents could draw some comfort from this.

"Well, Gentlemen," Lestrade began as he seated himself behind his desk, "I do hope you have managed to discover something that might help us bring these outrages to an end. I am loath to admit it, but we at the Yard have made little progress, other than to increase the number of officers who will scour Whitechapel tonight in anticipation of another killing."

"If our enquiries of today bring the results that I am hoping for, Lestrade, there will be no more victims."

The inspector smiled, I thought disbelievingly. "Is this the good news you gentlemen have brought me this morning? That would be a weight off my mind, I can tell you."

"Not quite," Holmes said, "but I may be able to clarify a related incident that you will have heard of by now. I would speculate that you have received a report of a stolen coach in Whitechapel last night. The coachman will have been found murdered or badly injured, and the conveyance itself not far away with either a dead man holding the reins or traces of blood on the cabby's seat."

Lestrade's eyes narrowed suspiciously as he picked up a sheet of paper from a pile awaiting his attention. "We have had such a report, from a constable on the early beat thereabouts. A coachman was found strangled near the corner of Commercial Street and Wentworth Street, and was identified from the contents of his pockets. A different officer discovered four wandering horses harnessed to a brougham in Hanbury Street, off Brick Lane, with a corpse leaning from the driver's seat. We later recognised him as Saul Naughton, a cove we have had our eye on for some time. But how did you come to know of this?"

Holmes related the events of the previous evening, while the inspector listened attentively.

"Thank you Mister Holmes," he said at last. "That explains these incidents satisfactorily. I am pleased to see that Doctor Watson and yourself escaped unhurt." He stretched wearily in his chair. "We must be thankful for small mercies, I suppose – we can close the file on Naughton now, but we are no nearer to finding this murderer who cuts out women's hearts." A sudden thought struck him. "Mr Holmes, could it be, since we are concerned with hearts here, that there is some sort of romantic intention involved. A suitor whose advances were spurned, perhaps?"

My friend raised his eyebrows. "That is certainly a new and interesting line of enquiry, Lestrade, and I wish you well with it. As for Watson and myself, our efforts may yet bear fruit before long and we will without fail inform you at once."

#

After an indifferent luncheon at a nearby coffee-house, we eventually set foot in Brick lane. It was a thoroughfare of no less depressing appearance than the rest of Whitechapel, and Doctor Venables free clinic for the underprivileged was situated on the corner of Brick Lane and Thrawl Street, almost opposite the Frying Pan Public House.

"Doubtlessly, these premises were formerly a shop of some description," said Holmes as we entered. A long queue of dirty urchins, impoverished women holding babies and men in various bandaged or damaged states glared at us suspiciously as we strode past them. They thought, no doubt, that we sought to obtain treatment ahead of them, and the babble of conversation took on a sinister note.

Holmes seemed oblivious to this, and we quickly reached a battered desk where a well-dressed short grey-haired man sat. He held a stethoscope against the chest of a pitifully thin elderly beggar.

"There is perhaps some small improvement," the doctor observed. "but if you persist in this excessive use of tobacco I can promise nothing but more difficulty with your respiration."

The patient grunted something which may have been thanks, and stumbled away. The doctor turned to beckon the next ailing person, and saw us for the first time.

"To what do I owe this honour, gentlemen?"

I could not tell if there was a hint of sarcasm in his voice, nor if disapproval had entered his expression. He had the face of a kindly man, as suggested by his service here, but it was also the face of a man besieged by worry. He made no effort to shake our hands.

"My name is Sherlock Holmes," began my friend, "and this is my friend and colleague, Doctor John Watson."

Doctor Venables nodded. "I have heard of you, Mr Holmes, but I fail to see anything to attract a consulting detective, here."

"We are here because both victims in the recent Whitechapel murders regularly received treatment from you. It occurred to me that you may be able to furnish some information."

The stethoscope swung against the doctor's chest as he turned away, but not before I saw the alarm in his eyes, as Holmes would have done. "I cannot imagine that I could supply anything relevant. If I have, the official force will doubtlessly recognise it."

"We are working with Scotland Yard," I remarked.

His gaze met mine for an instant, almost contemptuously, before returning to Holmes. "I have read of these crimes in the newspapers but, I repeat, I can tell you nothing more. Those women were among the many unfortunate patients I administer to. Why, in any case would anyone commit murders and remove the hearts of the victims? It is in the nature of some barbaric ritual."

"Why, indeed," Holmes agreed. He glanced at the small framed photographic portrait, which was among the books and bottles on the desk. "I presume that lady to be your wife, doctor?"

The alarm returned to Doctor Venables' eyes. "Are you of her acquaintance, sir?"

"I am unsure. She resembles greatly a nurse who cared for me in a Liverpool hospital."

"Then it cannot have been her. She has never been to Liverpool, nor was she ever employed as a nurse."

"Clearly I am mistaken. That quite settles it."

Doctor Venables glared at us impatiently. "And now I must ask you to excuse me. As you see, I have many patients waiting."

#

The glitter in Holmes' eyes told me he had been set upon a new scent. As he closed the clinic door behind us, I asked him how we were to proceed.

"The nearest telegraph office of course, Watson."

“To report to Lestrade?”

“To seek his confirmation on a vital point.”

I thought back. “Holmes, I believe I have it. Doctor Venables mentioned that the victims were found with their hearts cut out, yet Lestrade told us previously that this information was to be withheld to avoid panic. Am I correct?”

My friend beamed at me. “You progress constantly, Watson. If the good inspector confirms that this information is still restricted, then we have our first solid indication that we are on the right track.”

We turned a corner, to discover a dusty little Post Office between a hardware shop and a cobbler’s workplace. Holmes returned in minutes.

“I have instructed the Postmaster to look for us here. I do not think the reply will be long in coming.”

We walked a few paces to where a bench was situated near a horse trough, and seated ourselves.

“Holmes,” I said, to break the silence of a few minutes, “why did you ask after Doctor Venables’ wife? I see no connection with our enquiries.”

“You have evidently realised that my remarks were a ruse, old fellow, and you are quite right. It was a long shot, but quite worthwhile.”

“I am afraid you have confounded me.”

“It is simplicity itself. I observed Doctor Venables’ response to the mention of the Whitechapel victims, and became immediately convinced that he knew more of this affair than he was prepared to confide. A reference to his wife also brought a reaction. Once I had ascertained that the lady in the photograph was indeed his wife I asked myself if she could have ceased to care for him, bearing in mind his usual kindly nature and obvious continuing affection for her. A glance at his shirt supplied the answer."

"I confess that I noticed nothing."

"That is because you were not seeking the signs that I was convinced were there. A wife does not neglect her husband to the extent that his collar is worn in a soiled condition unless they are estranged, or unless she is unable to do otherwise."

"She could be ill. But you believe, I think, that she is restrained against her will?"

"I had expected something of the sort, to explain Doctor Venables' reluctance to assist us. It is not he who is committing these murders in Whitechapel, but he is being forced to collude in some way."

I was about to ask a further question when a man appeared in the doorway of the Post Office. He looked up and down the street and, on seeing us, approached with a yellow envelope which he handed to Holmes.

My friend ripped it open as the man retreated, and drew out the form from within.

"Is it as you suspected, Holmes?"

His face was grim as he thrust the paper into his pocket. "Just so. I fear we will have to forego dinner for a few hours."

#

Darkness had begun to fall as we took refuge in a convenient doorway, within sight of Doctor Venables' clinic. Every few minutes, and sometimes at longer intervals, a bedraggled figure would emerge and trudge away in one direction or another.

"This doctor cannot be a bad fellow, Holmes, since he keeps long hours at this place, in addition to his work in Harley Street."

"That has yet to be definitely determined. It is a matter, I think, of degree."

"What are you expecting to happen?" I asked.

"Very soon now, the last patient will leave. Then, if my theory is correct, Doctor Venables will visit the man who has enlisted his aid by force. There is but one such that I have heard of, who I am convinced is behind these new murders. I believe I know his name from references in my index, but not his motives. I hope to learn these, and to bring an end to these crimes, before this night is out."

I knew it to be useless to question my friend further. As was always his custom, he would tell me that which he wished me to know at his chosen time after the case was concluded. I sensed the mounting excitement in him as full darkness set in.

"Ah!" He exclaimed. "The doctor is locking the shop. Now, let us see which direction he chooses."

The road had been mostly quiet until now. A succession of hansoms appeared, some of them slowing down in the hope of a fare from the walking doctor. He ignored all of them, his gaze fixed straight ahead and his stride brisk. A landau and a four-horse brougham passed by before Holmes spoke again.

"We must proceed with utmost care, Watson. At all costs he must not see us."

The darkness assisted us greatly. The streets were poorly lit, some of the lamps without light completely, and we were able to stay fairly close to the physician as he left street after street behind.

In Mile End Street, near Ducking Pond Lane, a black square structure loomed out of the darkness. Doctor Venables entered it unhesitatingly, and Holmes put a hand on my shoulder.

"A warehouse, formerly for imported carpets. That smell is hessian, I think."

We held back for some minutes before approaching. As we drew nearer it became apparent that the place was disused, but had not been so for long. The exterior, such as we could see, was uncared for, its timber warped.

"Careful, Watson."

Holmes gripped the handle, and to our surprise the door opened easily. We drew our weapons and entered a dark passage leading to a vast open space. Voices could be heard from far off.

We reached the end of the passage and I thought my heart would stop as I felt Holmes stiffen next to me. Hanging before us, seemingly suspended on nothing, was the body of a young woman. Her long hair swirled slowly about her head as if she were a mermaid beneath the sea.

"She is quite dead," Holmes whispered as our surprise passed. "Immersed in formaldehyde, or a similar preservative."

"You do not seem surprised," I said in an equally low voice.

"You see before you the reason for the resurgence of the Whitechapel murders. But look beyond."

"This is a laboratory, Holmes! I have seldom seen so much equipment used in such a manner."

"For what has been attempted here, nothing less would have sufficed."

Then the voices came again, that of Doctor Venables rising to a high pitch.

"But you promised! You fiend, you gave me your word!"

A figure bathed in shadow, facing the doctor, replied in tones that chilled my blood. "I cannot release her to you until I am sure. If the procedure fails I will need you again. I can only trust you, Venables, while I have the power to compel you to obey me."

"But I went to great lengths to assure you, before I bought this place and the equipment, that this could never succeed. Medicine cannot do the work of God. If a life is taken, it cannot be retrieved. If there is any humanity left in you, let me take Marguerite and leave here. I have promised to keep silent."

The figure moved into the pool of light from the surrounding oil-lamps. I could make out a shock of light hair and a face that could have been hewn from stone. He was of average height and moved clumsily, but it was his voice that marked him as different. A pitiless drone, it held no emotion.

"And what if the first two attempts fail? What if Leonora remains in death? No, I must have fresh material to replace that which has failed her. I will continue until I succeed. She must live again."

In that vast space I heard a sob escape Doctor Venables. Holmes and I moved slowly and silently around the perimeter until we stood close to both men, still unseen. My friend chose that moment to intervene.

"Good evening, Mister Tiberius Fell."

Both men went still with shock, but Fell recovered first.

"I know not who you are, sir, nor what your right is to be here, but you are addressing Doctor Fell."

"I think not. You were dismissed from the Medical Council, despite your considerable qualifications, for conducting experiments that are forbidden."

"I was discharged by unimaginative fools, men who have no vision."

"But you served the late Professor Moriarty well, I understand, by attending to his wounded henchmen on occasion, after battles with the police."

Fell looked as if he would explode with anger. "That man was a genius, almost such as myself. What do you know of him?"

"I was there at his death. My name is Sherlock Holmes."

"You are Holmes!" A pistol appeared in Fell's hand and he began firing as he shouted hysterically: "You will not prevent Leonora's return to me. I will place a new heart in her breast and she will live. She is the only woman I have ever loved."

I had a glimpse of Doctor Venables scurrying for cover behind a tall cabinet. Sheltered by a wide pillar, Holmes and I prepared to return Fell's fire. That the man was quite mad I was convinced, for he raved in a maniacal voice as he discharged his weapon around him in random directions. His shouts had become incoherent, as a splintering of glass preceded a great deluge of liquid that washed across the floor behind us.

Fell went suddenly statue-still and dropped his pistol, and we continued to hold our fire. We watched in strange fascination as he ran towards the shattered glass case, kneeling among the fragments and the wetness of the floor to embrace the body that had fallen, forever lifeless, from it.

"Let him have a few moments," Holmes said as Doctor Venables emerged to join us. "There is a room back there where I think your wife has been held," my friend told him. "It would be as well to take her home. You may expect a visit from Inspector Lestrade, later."

Without a word, Doctor Venables made off in the direction that Holmes had indicated. A terrible wailing, an inhuman sound, that had issued from Fell's mouth ceased. A look of sudden comprehension filled Holmes' face and he turned to me urgently.

"Quickly, Watson."

But it was to no avail. The instant that I saw Fell lying there, I knew it was too late.

"Prussic acid," I explained to my friend. "Concealed on his person, I imagine."

"Another file that Lestrade can safely close."

"I cannot believe that a man well versed in medicine would aspire to something so impossible," I retorted. "Medicine will not allow for the heart of one person to be extracted and placed in the body of another. Nor, I suspect will it ever. It seems to me, Holmes, closer to witchcraft than science."

"The achievements yet to come, remain as yet unknown to us," he replied. "I first suspected that Fell was behind the new Whitechapel murders when I saw in my index that he was barred from his profession for conducting some quite bizarre procedures of his own invention. At one of the London hospitals he was discovered trying to stitch the severed arm of a corpse to the body of some poor fellow whose own arm had recently been amputated.

From there he eventually entered the service of the late Professor Moriarty, as you heard. After the professor's death he fled to Germany, where he met, became obsessed with and married Leonora von Buhler, the remains of whom you see before you. She died of an ailing heart shortly after the couple returned to this country, and that is when Fell must have sought out Doctor Venables, who he knew from his training days at Oxford."

"In order to abduct the doctor's wife." I ventured.

"Precisely. Having accomplished this, he was able to prevail upon Venables for his equipment and everything else he required. I presume that Fell had contracted some form of madness, to have conducted himself in such a manner, and the source of the victims of the original Whitechapel murderer was a convenience for him."

"So Lestrade was wrong. There was no connection, other than that, to the former crimes?"

He nodded. "So we have discovered, although the inspector's conclusions were understandable. I suppose, Watson, that it is necessary to report to that good fellow before returning to Baker Street. But cheer up, old friend, I am sure that Mrs Hudson has kept your dinner piping hot."

Suddenly, the dancers were still. Lord St Simon looked down from the balcony as the orchestra struck up another waltz. Many of his guests, invited to his home for his birthday celebrations, threaded themselves around the numerous tables to take to the dance floor.

It was only right, he thought, that a man of his social standing should surround himself with his equals at a time such as this, although he was normally averse to crowds, so that the occasion became as memorable as it should be. It was good to think that he had so many friends and relatives here tonight. He returned to his bedroom briefly, to ensure that his valet had made no error in dressing him. Before the mirror he appeared a fine figure, he thought, if a little stooped. True, his hair was tinged with grey now, and not as thick on the crown as it had been in his youth but, he decided, he had retained the aristocratic bearing that was a natural feature of all men of breeding. Was there a trace of foppishness in the new evening clothes he saw reflected? How could there be, when the style was his own invention? Had not his tailor complimented him on his exquisite taste and skill of design? The conclusion was inescapable: his appearance was immaculate. There was no room for improvement.

He descended the wide staircase slowly, so that his guests would have plenty of time to admire him before rushing to him with their congratulations. After many of them did that he became bored with the ritual and encouraged the dancing to continue, while he sat at his table for a while to drink champagne.

Among the throng of revolving dancers he was delighted to see a women he had previously noticed from the balcony, dancing past in the embrace of a young man who was a stranger to him.

Louise, Countess of Glenderbury, was his first cousin, and he had not seen her for two years. He watched until the dance came to an end. The music finished and Louise disengaged herself. She and her partner bowed briefly to each other and he turned away to be quickly lost from sight among the crowd. Lord St Simon was glad to see her making her way across the floor to his table.

"Robert," she said, smiling as she sat down in the vacant chair opposite him. "I'm sorry that we didn't meet as I arrived. I have so been looking forward to seeing you again. It's been more than two years, you know."

"My dear," Lord St Simon stretched his arm across the table to clasp her hand affectionately. "Where does the time go? You look so well." But she, too, had aged, he thought. She must be approaching her forties, by now.

"As do you, Robert. I wish you the happiest of birthdays."

"Thank you, my dear. But tell me, is all well at Braeloch House?"

"Well," She twirled a stray lock of blonde hair with her finger. "I run the estate as best I can. It has been suggested to me several times that I begin repairs to the parts of the house that have not stood the test of time, but my heart is not in it."

"You always had little affection for the place." He let his eyes rove quickly around the ballroom, while he thought of something new to say. Lord St Simon had never been entirely at ease with women. "I say, my dear," he began, not without embarrassment, "I expected you to be engaged, by now. The newspapers were full of you and a fellow called – what was his name – Julian Stonebridge."

She laughed. "We went to the races together, and to a society ball, I think. I am a widowed noblewoman, past the first flush of her youth, and you know how newspapers seize on such things. If I had been seen in public with him once more, they'd have posted the banns."

"Nothing came of it, then?"

"Good heavens, no."

Lord St Simon caught the attention of a passing waiter, and instructed him to bring another bottle of champagne, together with a glass for his cousin. When this was done, she said suddenly:

"But what of you, Robert? It distressed me to hear of the events that followed your wedding."

He was silent for a moment. The dancing had ceased and the orchestra finished playing, but now it struck up again and movement resumed as if at a sudden command. He glanced around briefly, noticing that the shadows cast by the gas chandeliers and oil lamps altered the expressions of men and women alike. Smiles became evil leers, and frowns were concentrated glares of intent.

"The American woman," he turned back to her at last. "an unfortunate incident that would have been best avoided. She was not really of our sort, and she is rarely in my thoughts now."

"Just as well, I would think. There are, as they say, many fish in the sea. I know of several fine families with daughters who are to enter the social circuit this coming summer."

"I am no longer the young man I once was," he smiled, and dismissed the subject.

She look a long drink and, not for the first time, he saw a hint of anxiety in her face. He refilled her glass and made a casual remark about one of the other guests. It was a joke, but her laughter in response was hollow.

"My dear," he began. "I am not the most sensitive of men, nor the most observant, but neither am I blind. It seems apparent that something troubles you, your eyes tell me as much, and if you could bring yourself to confide in me there is the possibility that I could help."

She looked at him silently, her expression haunted.

"Is it money?" he prompted.

More than a minute dragged by, before she was able to answer. "No, Robert. Not money."

"What, then?"

"I believe I am going mad."

He smiled sympathetically. "Whatever can you mean by that?"

"I…" She fell silent at once as someone walked past their table. The music was louder now, and she realised that a quiet conversation would be difficult. "Can we talk in private, please?"

Lord St Simon got to his feet and held her chair for her. "The library is the place."

They walked past the tables arranged at the edge of the room. Some of these had been deserted for the dance floor but other guests, mostly elderly, sat watching and drinking. He opened a stout oak door that led into a flagstoned corridor, then another that brought them to a large gas-lit room that was lined with leather-bound volumes.

"Sit here, my dear. We will not be disturbed." He seated her at a reading-table and placed himself opposite.

"No one will hear us?" She asked with tears in her eyes.

“No one. Now, what is this nonsense about madness?”

“It is not nonsense, Robert, or I would not have troubled you with it. There have been three incidents within the last two weeks in which I must have participated, and yet I did not.”

He raised his eyebrows. “That sounds a most curious situation.”

“It is one that has terrified me, to the point where I am becoming frantic. Four days ago I took the trap to Inverness, to see Mr Whemple. Do you remember him?”

“The Solicitor?”

She nodded. “I had some small matter regarding the estate to settle. Imagine my shock when he referred to a previous visit when I transferred one thousand acres of Braeloch land to a Mr Thomas Ingolby.”

“But you knew nothing of this?”

“Not of the transaction nor of the buyer. I have never heard of such a man.”

“That is extraordinary.” Lord St Simon looked puzzled but interested. “Did Whemple state that you actually signed the papers in his presence?”

“He did, and produced them for me to scrutinize. The signature was my own. Nor is that the end of the story. Still dismayed by this unexplainable incident I called at my bank, which you may remember is the Scottish Landowners and Merchants, to arrange for a small pension to be paid to the widow of a recently-deceased footman, who had rendered long and faithful service. Mr Ogilvie, the manager, mentioned during our conversation in his office that the regular withdrawals from my personal account were proceeding as arranged. He saw at once that I had not received this news well, so much so that he became concerned and sent for a glass of water. I explained that I knew nothing of such an arrangement concerning my account, and the poor man seemed as shocked as I because, he insisted, I had confirmed it in that very room, no more than two weeks before."

"This is strange indeed. Was the date of the withdrawal mentioned?"

"There have been two. On Tuesday, and the same day of the following week."

"On the same day of the week, perchance, as the supposed land transfer?"

She nodded. "They both took place on the first Tuesday."

"May I ask, my dear, how much is involved?"

"Five thousand pounds, for each withdrawal."

"And to whom was the money credited?"

"It was released in cash, to a Mr Thomas Ingolby."

"The same recipient as the land transfer?"

"Yes," her voice rose, and he sensed the onset of panic. "Oh, Robert, what is happening to me? If I cannot remember my own recent actions, then I must be losing my mind. What else have I done that I cannot recollect? What am I to do?"

Lord St Simon rose and instinctively put his arm around her. He was not familiar with this sort of situation, nor comfortable with it, yet he had promised to help and so something had to be done.

“Now, now, my dear, you must calm yourself. It seems to me that there can be only two explanations for these curious events. Either you are suffering from some sort of illness, which I do not suspect for a moment, or someone, and I cannot imagine who or how, is impersonating you.”

“I have considered that but who would do such a thing, and how could it be done? How would they be able to duplicate my signature to the satisfaction of Mr Whemple and Mr Ogilvie, as well as assume my appearance? It all seems highly improbable.”

“Indeed it does,” he removed his arm now that she appeared to have regained herself, and went back to his chair, “but it occurs to me that there is a way to throw some light on the situation. You said that the bank withdrawals took place on two consecutive Tuesdays, did you not?”

“I did, but naturally I instructed Mr Ogilvie to discontinue them at once.”

“Of course, but Mr Ingolby, or whoever he is, will not know of that until he attempts to make the next one.”

Her face brightened. “You believe it might be possible to trap him?”

“It sounds to me likely. Have you consulted the police about any of this?”

“No, I wished to avoid the scandal that would come about, if it became common knowledge.” She looked away from him. “And I feared for my reputation. There are those hereabouts who would be only too willing to believe that I have become unbalanced.”

“There are always those who would rejoice at another’s misfortunes,” he observed. “However, I am quite sure that they will find nothing to gloat about here. Tuesday is the day after tomorrow, and until then I will be pleased if you will remain as a guest here. Then, at the appointed time, you and I, in the company of a constable, will wait in the bank for this mysterious thief, for he is no more than that, and he will be arrested. You may be sure that the police will get the truth out of him quickly, and so all your concerns will be dispelled."

#

The previous withdrawals from the account of the Countess of Glenderbury had been made within twenty minutes either side of mid-day. This, Lord St Simon was certain, was deliberate because the bank was most busy at that time.

As it happened, it was not a constable who was assigned to the case, since it was considered sufficiently serious for the attentions of Inspector McKay of the Inverness Detective Division, a tall, dour Scotsman whose past successes were not inconsiderable.

Tuesday arrived and the three, the Inspector, the Countess and Lord St Simon, stood in a narrow gallery looking down upon the public side of the banking hall. Mid-day came and went, and several times the inspector started forward to get a better look over the gleaming brass rail as a new customer entered the building. Always it proved to be a false start, and he relaxed his posture and shook his head. At three o'clock the bank closed and they left, after apologising to Mr Ogilvie for any disruption or inconvenience they may have caused.

"Our robber seems to have changed his mind," the inspector said to Lord St Simon and the Countess, "but we'll be keeping an eye on the case, never fear."

Lord St Simon thanked him in an off-hand manner, and dismissed him.

"I can see no other approach to this," Louise said as they watched the inspector walk away. "I am sorry that I involved you, Robert. It came to nothing, after all."

"I am not one to give up so easily. After all, this man's villainy has cost you a tidy sum. And there is the question of the land and the anxiety that you have suffered at his hands." He considered briefly. "There is a Post Office a little way along this street, I noticed it as we arrived. A telegram may bring us some results."

She looked at him anxiously. "I would not have this spread afar, Robert. We were careful to tell the inspector no more than we felt he needed to know."

"I am thinking of the fellow who found Hatty Doran, the American woman, for me, when she disappeared after our marriage. He seemed quite able, if a little high-handed for his station. I was told that he is experienced in such matters."

"If you are sure of his discretion then, perhaps he could make some enquiries. I remember that he lives in London, but what is his name?"

"To the best of my recollection, it is Sherlock Holmes."

#

It was well into the afternoon of the following day, when the housekeeper, Mrs Hudson, showed Lord St Simon and Louise, Countess of Glenderbury, into an upstairs room in Baker Street.

They had a glimpse of a tall thin man, draped across an armchair while reading a newspaper, before he rose as they were announced. He bowed to them and Lord St Simon introduced his cousin.

"Pray take the other armchair and the basket chair," said Sherlock Holmes after acknowledging them. "Allow me to call for some tea."

"Do not do so on our account," Lord St Simon answered. "We have little time before returning to Scotland by the early evening train."

"Very well. How then, can I assist you?"

Making no reference to their previous encounter, Lord St Simon described the events which so troubled his cousin. Except for an occasional nod and to give a brief answer to confirm his account, the Countess remained silent.

When this was over, Sherlock Holmes remained in the position he had adopted throughout. He sat leaning forward with his elbows on his knees, supporting his chin. His eyes were closed and his visitors looked at each other wondering if he had fallen asleep, until he slowly sat up straight in his chair.

"You realise, of course, that this is the work of someone very close to you?"

"I have arrived at that conclusion," Lord St Simon agreed. "This must be so, because of the familiarity displayed by whoever is responsible with facets of my cousin's life. For example, he knew which solicitor and bank she customarily uses."

"Quite so. Also they – there must be two at least, since we are apparently dealing with a woman who resembles the Countess, as well as the man called Ingolby – were able to obtain and reproduce her signature." Holmes turned to the Countess. "Did you obtain an address from the bank or the solicitor? Ingolby must have left one in order to complete the transactions."

"We did." Louise replied in an uncharacteristically subdued voice. "A groom was despatched there to identify the place. He found nothing but an open field."

"That is highly significant! If the trail ends so quickly, and so obviously, then it surely means that they are not afraid of their actions until now being discovered. There is more to this, I think, than the fraudulent obtaining of a piece of land and the sum of ten thousand pounds."

"Who could be doing this?" she pleaded anxiously.

"How many staff are employed at Braeloch?" Holmes asked.

"The immediate staff number only four, since the house is now much smaller than it once was. Much of it now lies in ruins, but the west wing and some of the main structure are still inhabited. We have a number of under-maids, kitchen staff and the like, but I rarely see them."

"Pray describe the four you mentioned."

Louise shifted nervously in her seat. "Our housekeeper, the woman who sees to the overall running of Braeloch, is Rosemary Trafford. She is a tall, elderly spinster who has been with us for many years. Montcreiff, the butler, is a young man, quite intelligent, who has only five years' service but has so far been satisfactory. Anna Birtles, the head kitchen maid, is short and young to hold such a post, barely out of her teens I would think, but has proved herself highly efficient. She is small for her age with coal-black hair. The last of the four is the coachman, Buchanan. He is old and half-crippled, poor man, but still serves us well. He, also, has been with us since my father's time."

For several minutes, Holmes appeared lost in thought.

"I have but one more question," he said then, addressing them both. "When the arrangement was made to wait at the bank with Inspector McKay, did you confide your intention to anyone else?"

They paused for a moment, glancing at each other and shaking their heads.

"Not I," Lord St Simon said.

"Nor I," the Countess answered.

"Not by the written word, perhaps in a letter to a friend or relation?"

Louise's expression changed, as if she had suddenly realised the importance of something hitherto considered trivial.

Holmes saw this at once. "Countess, I beg you to be frank with me. The more you disclose, the greater my chance of unravelling this affair."

She avoided the eyes of both men. "I noted the arrangement, in the diary I keep concerning the estate."

"This was in advance of the event?"

"Two days before, when Robert suggested it."

Lord St Simon looked at her in mild surprise, and Holmes continued.

"Is your diary kept in a secure or hidden place, known to yourself only?"

"Not at all. It lies in the drawer of my writing-desk. There is no lock, nor has there ever been a need for one."

"That is quite clear." Holmes reached for his Bradshaw and consulted it briefly. "I see that there is an early train for Inverness, tomorrow. I should be able to attend an interview with Inspector McKay by mid-afternoon."

"You must stay at Braeloch!" The Countess exclaimed, but Lord St Simon's disapproving glance did not go unnoticed by Holmes.

"Thank you, Countess," he replied, "but I find that an investigation invariably proceeds more quickly if I keep myself at a distance. No, an inn, I think, will suffice."

"Do you think you can conclude this quickly?" Lord St Simon enquired.

"I will give it my full attention. At this early stage, I can promise no more." Holmes rose to his feet. "But now I see that time has overtaken us, and I still have much to do. If there is nothing further I will detain you no longer, other than to say that it has been my honour and pleasure to meet you both. Be assured that you will hear from me at Braeloch, before long."

The Countess, looking somewhat relieved, was effusive in her thanks, while Lord St Simon grunted something that could have been an acknowledgement. Holmes bowed and opened the door, calling for Mrs Hudson to show them out.

From the window, he watched as they summoned a hansom and left Baker Street. After a few moments he settled himself in an armchair and filled his clay pipe with tobacco from the Persian slipper. He reflected that this would not be a three-pipe problem, but was not without its points of interest.

#

"I received a telegram from the Countess of Glenderbury, informing me that I was to expect you," Inspector McKay said disapprovingly.

“I am not here to interfere with your investigation, Inspector, but to conduct my own at the request of the Countess and her cousin, Lord St Simon.”

“We are not usually partial to amateurs here in Scotland, Mr Holmes, but I am told that you have helped Lord St Simon, before now.”

“It was, in fact, he who recommended me to his cousin.”

The inspector lit a cigarette, after offering one to Holmes, who declined. “So I understand. Also, Scotland Yard seem to look upon you favourably.”

“On occasion, I have been of some trifling assistance to the official force.”

“What then, can I tell you of this affair? Let me say at once that, although I do not of course doubt the account I have been given by the Countess, I have not been able to trace anyone who is likely to have impersonated her.”

Holmes glanced thoughtfully around the inspector’s office. “And there have been no further attempts to withdraw money from the Countess’s bank account?”

“None. I have had a man stationed inside the bank, but without result.”

“Has anything unusual occurred, on the Braeloch estate?”

McKay looked surprised. “I don’t know how you could have suspected such a thing, Mr Holmes, but the gamekeeper there shot an intruder in the grounds, last night.”

“Is the intruder dead?”

“He is.”

Holmes nodded. "Is he known?"

"He has yet to be identified."

"No doubt he will be, shortly. Inspector, from your visits to Braeloch, can you recall whether the staff live on or near the premises?"

McKay rose to his feet and paced the length of the room awkwardly, as if beset by cramp. "As I remember, most of the staff live away. Exceptions are the butler of course, Buchanan the coachman, the girl who runs the kitchen and a few of the under-maids, who have their quarters in a separate building near the entrance gate."

"Thank you, Inspector." Holmes stood up and they shook hands. "But now it is getting late, and I have yet to see the Countess's solicitor and her bank manager, if I can catch them. Should you require me for any reason, you will most probably find me at the inn near the town Hall. I believe it is called 'The Highland Lassie'.

#

Four days passed, before Holmes despatched a telegram to Braeloch to inform the Countess that he would be calling on her in the afternoon. He spent the morning in his room at the inn, smoking and turning over in his mind everything that he had learned since his arrival in Inverness.

By mid-day, he had received no reply to indicate that his proposed visit would be inconvenient and so, after a lunch of local trout, he settled with the innkeeper and took a passing hansom to the Countess's ancestral home.

It proved to be a pleasant journey. The sky was an almost cloudless blue and the air was clear, if a little chilly. Birds sang as the city was left behind and tree-lined roads stretched ahead. After a while the driver turned the hansom into the short approach to tall ornamental gates which were opened immediately, and they passed the gatekeeper's lodge and maid's quarters that stood at the beginning of the long gravel drive.

The house, which appeared suddenly after a cluster of tall elms, was a low curved structure. Almost half of it, he could see, had fallen into a state of disrepair. The only sign of life was the smoke which hung in a vertical stream in the still air from several of the many tall chimneys. Holmes dismissed the hansom and the wide studded door opened as he approached the steps. The butler who admitted him was young, with quick sharp movements. Montcreiff, he presumed.

Holmes was showed into a cavernous room. Three tall curtained windows dominated one wall, and gave an almost panoramic view of the grounds and distant lake. As the door was closed behind him, he saw that a fire had been lit in the grate and that chairs and a chaise-longue were arranged near it. The Countess and Lord St Simon sat waiting.

"Your telegram gave us little notice, Mr Holmes," Lord St Simon said without any greeting.

"Robert," the Countess protested. "Is the loss of an afternoon's shooting worth more than my peace of mind?"

"Of course not, my dear," her cousin replied with some embarrassment.

"I understood," said Holmes, "that this was a matter of some concern to you."

Lord St Simon raised his head, in a superior fashion. "Very well, then. What have you discovered?"

"Please tell us, Mr Holmes," the Countess said anxiously. "I must know the truth of this."

"Have you solved it?" Lord St Simon asked impatiently.

"I have."

Lord St Simon started to say, "Then out with it, man", but stopped immediately when confronted with Holmes' steely gaze. With enforced patience, he glanced at his cousin and sat back in his chair.

"This explanation," Holmes began after the Countess had bade him be seated, "begins more than thirty-five years ago. I regret, Countess, that you may find some of it unpleasant."

"Nevertheless," she acknowledged, "pray continue."

Holmes took a moment to consider his words. "I am sorry to tell you that, about that time, your mother, Lady Catriona, bore a second child, though your father had by then passed away."

"Impossible!" Lord St Simon exploded, his face reddening. "How dare you suggest this, sir!"

"I dare because I am merely repeating what is a matter of official record. This information is from the Registry of Births, Marriages and Deaths, here in Inverness. I spent several hours there, authenticating my suspicions."

"Outrageous! There is an error in your findings."

The Countess shook her head slowly, wearing an expression of absolute surprise. "She never told me."

"I think not," Holmes continued, in reply to Lord St Simon. "The birth was of course concealed, apart from the attending physician insisting upon its registration. The father, a coachman, was paid for his silence and the child, a girl called Flora, was eventually adopted. There was a report that she died, but I was able to disprove it."

"Then I have a sister, or at least a half-sister," the Countess whispered in astonishment. "My mother took the secret to her grave."

"Indeed, and Flora herself now has a daughter, who is known to you."

"Then who is she?" Lord St Simon interrupted.

"That will soon become clear, but let me continue. The family who adopted Flora were without children of their own. The mother, an upright and righteous woman, died a few years later leaving the father and adopted daughter who grew to maturity and married. Flora's husband seems to have been an unscrupulous fellow, who knew of his wife's ancestry and with her harboured a strong desire to obtain at all costs those things that he believed to be their rightful inheritance. They eventually had a daughter of their own, who was brought up to believe that this was her sole purpose in life. He, however, can no longer pursue that aim, since your gamekeeper recently shot him as an intruder. His name was one that has lately become familiar to you. It was Thomas Ingolby."

Holmes paused in his narrative, to enable the Countess to absorb this.

"The name Mr Whemple told me of, and Mr Ogilvie," she said, wide-eyed.

"The same. I interviewed those gentlemen, and Flora's adoptive father, who has survived to a ripe old age. He was most helpful, and had always disapproved of Ingolby's intentions. When you came to me in Baker Street, I realised at once that your supposition that someone resembling you had been at work here must be correct, for how else could Mr Whemple and Mr Ogilvie have been approached? I disregarded the notion of an identical twin, since you would already have mentioned this or acted upon it. There remained then, two possibilities: your impersonator was either someone who could make themselves look like you, or someone who naturally resembled you, Countess. Eventually I realised that both these factors were relevant."

"But who is doing this?" Lord St Simon could no longer contain his impatience.

Holmes disregarded him, and continued. "You may have received a report from your staff, Countess, or you, Lord St Simon, may have as you are staying here, of a fellow of unruly appearance loitering nearby, along the road. There is no need for alarm at this, for it was I. My purpose was to observe the arrivals or departures of those of your staff who live elsewhere. I wished to see if any of the under-maids or others resembled you in any way."

"And did you think so, Mr Holmes?" the Countess asked in an uncertain voice.

"No, but I knew then that the person I sought lived within the estate. She has been regularly giving information, such as a specimen of your signature and the date when you were to visit the bank with Inspector McKay, to Thomas Ingolby, who trespassed on your land several times for the purpose of receiving it but was at last shot while leaving."

The Countess shook her head. "But there is no one here who bears such a resemblance."

"Ah, but there is, slight though it may be, but it is not she who is the impersonator. I recall that you mentioned that the girl you know as Anna Birtles is short, and so could not have carried out the deception."

“Anna!” The Countess cried in astonishment.

“Indeed,” Holmes confirmed. “Is she, by any chance, absent from her duties today?”

“Why yes, she appeared distraught, but would not reveal the cause.”

“Then let me suggest that it was because her father was killed by the gamekeeper. Has she been observed to act strangely in any way, lately?”

The Countess, reeling from these revelations, tried to recall any such incidents. “Recently,” she said after a few moments, “Anna was found in the kitchen during the early hours. She appeared to have been sleepwalking.”

“Or, more likely, I think, passing something of significance to her father. I discovered quite easily his point of entry, an improvised tunnel through a thick bush at the edge of the grounds.”

“But you still have not revealed the imposter,” a slightly becalmed Lord St Simon pointed out.

“Her identity became obvious after my conversation with Flora’s adoptive father. Also, he mentioned repeatedly the change in his daughter’s disposition, after she married Thomas Ingolby, to the extent that he disowned her. Under Ingolby’s influence she undertook to impersonate you, Countess, to the extent that both the solicitor and bank manager were deceived.”

“My half-sister? She must look much like me.”

“Not quite to the extent that she could pass for you. To confirm my suspicions I visited her home, she lives in a poor quarter on the other side of Inverness, while she and her husband were absent, and discovered a wig and theatrical make-up. From the papers in her desk I found that she was once a little-known actress, and from a photographic portrait that her facial structure was extremely similar to your own. This is not of course so surprising, since you both have the same mother, but her skilled enhancement made the resemblance close to identical. Afterwards, I deliberately encountered her in the street and explained that her crimes were known. If she is able to, after the shock of her husband's death, I imagine she has left the country by now. If that is not so, then Inspector McKay will doubtless add this affair to his record of successes, as he will with Anna's arrest."

"But what was the purpose of all this?"

"Mrs Flora Ingolby would not disclose it, but I imagine it was an attempt to have you hidden away somewhere as insane, and then for her to come forward to make some claim upon your estate. As I made clear to her, it was all planned and carried out in ignorance, for it had no chance of success. You need have no fear therefore, of any further strange experiences at their hands, nor of the effects of their current misdeeds. I have ensured that both Mr Whemple and Mr Ogilvie have the reversal of the false transactions well in hand."

"So," Lord St Simon remarked, "the situation has turned out to be quite simple, after all." He turned to his cousin. "I would, of course, have reached the same conclusion myself by the end of the day."

The Countess, still shocked by all that she had learned, gave him a doubtful glance and shook her head.

"Thank you, Mr Holmes," she said absently, in the tone of one who believes that she is dreaming.

"As for me," Holmes finished, "I must catch the London train that leaves Inverness in just over an hour. Perhaps I could prevail upon you for the use of a coach to the station? If not, then I have the pleasure of wishing you both good morning."

The Adventure of the Silent Sister

It was a beautiful June morning when Sherlock Holmes appeared for breakfast in high spirits. I had risen early and finished my breakfast, but offered immediately to call Mrs Hudson in order to accommodate my friend.

"Thank you, Watson, but that will not be necessary, for I have no appetite this morning," he replied in an almost light-hearted tone. "However, I see that our good lady has supplied an extra cup and that the remaining coffee in the pot is still hot, since that you have poured for yourself is steaming. That will suffice for me until lunch-time, I think."

"Your cases are progressing well then?" I asked as I poured the dark liquid for him. "You are rarely this cheerful in the morning."

He lowered himself into the chair opposite. "As it happens I have four current cases, all nearing successful conclusions."

"No wonder you are in such good spirits. Congratulations, old fellow."

I knew little about Holmes' recent activities, since a bout of influenza had prevented me from accompanying him for the past two weeks. A locum had maintained my practice, satisfactorily as far as I knew, and I was as yet unable to relieve him. Although past the contagion stage I still felt quite weak, and tired easily.

"What do you say to a leisurely walk in St James Park?" he asked unexpectedly as he emptied his cup and got to his feet.

“That would be very much to my liking,” was my puzzled reply. “But it is unusual for you to suggest such a thing, Holmes.”

He gestured towards the window. “It is a warm and windless day, and I expect no results from the enquiries I have made towards concluding my investigations until later in the week. What else would come to mind at such a time?”

“Your reasoning, as usual, is impeccable,” I laughed, elevating my mood to match his. “We have but to pick up our hats and canes as we leave, and shout to Mrs Hudson that she can now clear away our breakfast things, before strolling into the sunshine.”

We left our lodgings behind and walked along Baker Street, I moving a little more slowly than usual. By contrast Holmes was truly light-hearted today, seeming exhilarated by the very air he breathed.

”You know, Watson….,” he began as we neared a corner, then paused abruptly as a heavy-set man with a red beard suddenly accosted us.

“Sir,” the stranger addressed me breathlessly and in a concerned manner, “are you Mr Sherlock Holmes?”

We came to an immediate halt. “Not at all,” I replied, “but this is Mr Holmes.”

His attention switched to my friend. “Mr Holmes, thank God I caught you. I have urgent need of your services, if you will accept me as a client.”

“To that I may agree,” Holmes scrutinized the man carefully. “But first you must tell us of your circumstances. Allow me to introduce my friend and colleague, Doctor John Watson, whose assistance has often proved invaluable.”

Walking between us, the stranger identified himself. "My name is Septimus Todd," he began. "Inspector Lestrade of Scotland Yard recommended that I consult you."

"Most kind of him," Holmes suppressed a smile.

"I am desperately worried about my sister. She is a changed woman."

"Then are you certain that it is I who can be of assistance? If it is a question of altered behaviour there is most often a medical explanation, in which case Doctor Watson would be far more useful to you than I. Or, he may be able to recommend someone."

I felt immediate concern at the man's reaction to this. Tears came to his eyes and the depth of his emotion was apparent. "No sir, it is nothing like that. Since my dear wife passed away, some three years ago, Elinora has been all I have left in the world."

"She lives with you, I presume."

"That is correct. She has done so since soon after Margaret's passing, and looks after me completely. She dismissed the servants, saying that their services were an unnecessary expense, and so it has proved to be."

Holmes nodded. "Mr Todd, you are clearly upset. Watson and I are about to walk in St James Park. You are welcome to join us. Please feel free to tell us your story, when you are able."

We progressed south for quite a while in silence, until Holmes finally spoke. "Mr Todd, we are now entering The Mall, and will soon be approaching St James Park. I suggest you use the time until we reach there to calm yourself and to collect your thoughts, then after we arrive you can relate your problem from its beginning in that peaceful setting so that we can decide your best course of action."

We entered the park a short while later, and soon came upon a long bench near the lake, where pelicans, swans and other water-fowl swam freely in their perpetual hunt for food. We sat, Mr Todd still clearly distressed.

"Now," Holmes said to him, "if you would care to relate to us the nature of your sister's difficulties, we can arrive at a decision as to who can best help you. Pray be precise, leaving out not the smallest detail from the beginning."

Mr Todd stared at the lake for a moment, as if wondering where to begin, then he turned to us, having apparently decided.

"Elinora has always been a quiet girl," he began, "but with a quick mind. A few years ago she persuaded our father to pay for a course in mathematics at one of the minor universities. She was the only female in the class and endured some badgering from the others, but went on to silence her tormenters by obtaining the highest marks of them all. She would not speak of her objective in immersing herself in this knowledge, saying only that it was her insurance against poverty. Soon after the completion of her instruction, our father died.

"His estate, derived mostly from a Derbyshire coal mine which he sold during his final years, was divided equally between us. I invested heavily in gold stock, which has produced a reasonable living since, while my sister was persuaded by a friend to invest through several banks in a South African diamond mine which soon ceased to yield. Left almost penniless, she became my companion and housekeeper and ran things with an almost military precision. We lived together quite happily until she met a certain Mr Arnold Trent, through a friend from her weekly sewing circle. He began to court her, and although it seemed to me to be a rather cold relationship, I approved for her sake. Then a fellow I know from the Chamber of Commerce pointed him out to me in the street one day, as a man of doubtful character. I decided to learn something of Trent's past, and discovered a history of petty theft and attempted embezzlement. At this I acted at once to sever all connections with Mr Trent, though this naturally was the cause of much friction between my sister and myself, until she came to realise his true nature. Nevertheless, she was always a girl to take things very much to heart, and has not been the same towards me since despite the miserable life she would have had without my intervention. She is now constantly morose, and we exist in silence for much of the time we are together."

"Not unusual surely," I commented, "in the circumstances you describe."

"There is more to it than that, Doctor. One day she returned from Hampstead, we live quite close to the village, where she had ordered groceries. There she had chanced to meet one of her tutors from her university days, an elderly lady by the name of Elizabeth Heald."

"One moment," Holmes interrupted. "You have said that this man Trent has a dishonest reputation. What then, did you imagine was the reason for his courtship of your sister, as she was penniless and dependant on yourself for her living? Did you consider that his interest might have been genuine?"

"Not for an instant. From the description of his past activities that I received from various sources, I formed the opinion that he was most likely planning to use Elinora to somehow gain access to my finances. This would not have been the first time he had hatched such a plan."

"I understand. Pray continue."

"Elinora told me then that she and this Miss Heald had arranged to meet regularly every month, and she would stay with her for several days. When she returned from such meetings she was markedly evasive when I enquired about how they had spent their time. Usually she would continue the silence which had by now become normal between us, but on more than one occasion she conveniently claimed to have no memory of whatever transpired. I doubted the truth of this, but at the mention of such lapses I became seriously worried. I insisted, much against her protests, that she seek medical help. Several doctors have examined her and discovered nothing amiss, and her only comment was to shrug off my concern and make light of it, saying that no harm could come of her continuing to see Miss Heald."

"What did you do then?" I asked.

Our new acquaintance moved restlessly in his seat. "I convinced myself that Trent's hand was in this, somewhere. Remembering his past, I consulted Scotland Yard with my suspicions that my sister was being drawn into something of a criminal nature. Inspector Lestrade concluded that nothing could be done, since no crime had yet been committed, but suggested that I enlist your assistance for my own peace of mind."

"Hence your arrival at Baker Street," my friend surmised.

"That did not follow immediately. It occurred to me that you might dismiss me in the same manner, and so I sought something to give credence to my fears. In her absence, I searched for and found the key to Elinora's desk. I was unsure what to look for, but in one of the drawers were papers from her university days, including the whereabouts of Miss Elizabeth Heald. Armed with this knowledge, I journeyed to Watford to see her, only to discover that her house is derelict and the lady passed away more than a year ago."

"This situation begins to have some interesting features," Holmes remarked.

"I am very relieved that you think so."

"Have you, by any chance, recorded the dates of your sister's meetings with this woman?"

"As it happens, I have. I did this to support my case, at Scotland Yard."

Holmes nodded. "When did these meetings begin?"

"The first was in February."

"So you have dates for February, March, April and May, presuming that this month's meeting has not yet taken place?"

"Not until now." Mr Todd drew a folded paper from his pocket. "The dates were, February 4th, 5th and 6th, March 13th, 14th and 15th, April 5th, 6th and 7th and May 18th, 19th and 20th."

Holmes threw a quick glance in my direction, to ensure that I had noted these.

"Three consecutive days, on each occasion. I must impress upon you, Mr Todd, the importance of informing me at once when the date of the next meeting becomes known to you. If you could do this in advance, it would be of immeasurable assistance."

"I undertake to communicate with you by telegraph, at the first possible moment, Mr Holmes. I cannot express adequately my relief that you have consented to come to my aid. You would have me continue as usual then, until the time of the next meeting becomes known to me?"

"Not at all." Holmes turned to our client wearing a mild expression. "I was about to suggest that Doctor Watson and myself accompany you to your home on some pretext, so that we can meet your sister this morning."

#

We left St James Park shortly afterwards. I flagged down a passing four-wheeler, and we found ourselves in Hampstead well before mid-day.

Mr Todd and his sister lived in a square, three-storey town house in a mews near the local parish church. Holmes had suggested that he introduce us as prospective investors in gold shares, in search of advice, and our client represented us as such to his sister. She was a tall slim woman who could have been attractive, but for her unvarying grim expression and her aura of sadness as she served us tea. Her dress was plain, almost funereal, and her black hair gleamed. I saw that her eyes were dull, presumably from the lasting pain of losing Mr Trent.

The conversation, during our short visit, proved to be sparse. Mr Todd spoke haltingly in the presence of his sister, but maintained the deception as to his connection with Holmes and myself.

I reflected, as we left, that she had hardly spoken a word to us.

"I have reminded Mr Todd again of the necessity of informing us immediately, the next time Miss Elinora prepares to attend such a meeting." Holmes hailed an approaching hansom. "I have also assured him that he will hear from us soon."

"But, if she seeks to conceal her movements, how is he to distinguish between her usual short absences for household matters and her next meeting with whoever she is seeing?"

"I suggested that he accompany her on each excursion. When her intention is to meet her mysterious friend, she will do all in her power to ensure that she makes the journey alone."

The next few days were largely uneventful. Apart from a thorough examination of his index, my friend occupied himself mainly with his endless chemical experiments. I continued to recover my strength, and began to consider the prospect of returning to my practice soon.

It was during the early evening of the 27th, that two telegrams arrived for Holmes. He received them eagerly, obviously relieved at this end to a period of monotony.

"At last, Watson!" he cried as he read the contents of the first. "One of my pending cases has finally come to fruition. If I enlist the help of the Yard tomorrow, a child should be restored to its parents and an abductor should be behind bars not long after mid-day."

"Excellent. The second telegram is doubtlessly a satisfactory conclusion to another pending affair."

He tore open the envelope, and I saw his expression change. "This is from Mr Todd. He is certain that his sister intends to embark on another meeting in the morning."

"That is of less importance than the other case, surely?"

"Not if my deductions are correct."

I cast my mind back. "When we returned from Mr Todd's house you spent much time consulting your index. Am I to assume that you learned something further?"

"You are indeed. If we are to prevent a serious crime, and possibly injuries to innocent people, it is essential that Miss Elinora Todd is observed when she ventures forth from their house tomorrow. Yet I am now bound to see this other matter through. I may be a detective of some standing, but I cannot be in two places at once."

“Barker has assisted you several times since the Josiah Amberley affair.”

“Which you have since dramatized out of all proportion for your readers.” His thin form paced the room restlessly, wrestling with indecision. “No, I have established that Barker is at present occupied in Newcastle, on a rather involved case of murder. I fear that I must search elsewhere.”

Without thinking, I said quickly. “Time was when you would have used my services for such as this, Holmes. They are still available to you.”

“My dear fellow!” he turned towards me at once. “I could not think of it. You are not yet recovered, and probably will lack the energy for some time. It is a pity though, your assistance here would have been invaluable.”

I sat up straight in my chair. “I have felt stronger, Holmes, these past four or five days. In fact I am at the point of deciding the date of my return to my practice. I would willingly delay this, if you think I can be useful.”

“Are you sure that you could undertake such a task? Were it not for your indisposition I would have thought of you at once, but I would not delay your recovery for the world.”

“I am certain, yet something has just come to mind that precludes such a course.”

A quick smile passed over his hawk-like features. “I can imagine no such thing, in the face of your enthusiasm.”

“But the lady knows me from our visit to see her, with Mr Todd. I have not your expertise at following people, and would quickly be noticed.”

To my great surprise, Holmes threw back his head and laughed.

"Give that not a moment of consideration, my good friend. I assure you, that is the least of our worries."

#

I was to discover, after being roused from my bed early the next morning, why my friend was unconcerned. As soon as Mrs Hudson had reclaimed the breakfast things, he revealed his strategy.

"Do me the kindness of sitting in that upright chair, Watson. I am about to make you invisible to anyone you might care to follow."

With that he hastily wound a towel around my neck and produced the case containing his theatrical make-up that I had seen him use often with great effect. I closed my eyes as he brushed my face lightly and applied some of the contents of several jars and bottles. Finally, he placed a grey wig on my head and stood back to admire his work. After a critical appraisal he appeared satisfied and held a mirror in front of my face. The image I saw reflected was of an older man, who did not resemble John Watson in the least.

"And so, old fellow, you will be able to pursue Miss Elinora Todd with impunity. I think that even your patients would not recognise you without difficulty."

"It does not surprise me that no disguise of yours has ever failed."

He nodded. "We have no way of knowing at what time Miss Elinora will set out, therefore it would be as well to be waiting near the house early. I wish you well, Watson. As always, I know there is no one I can more safely depend upon. Goodbye, old fellow, until we meet here again later."

Moments later I found myself in a hansom on my way to Hampstead. On arrival I instructed the cabby to wait near some overhanging trees within sight of the house. At first he seemed suspicious of my motives but I implied, rather than stated, that I was connected to Scotland Yard. My vigil was not a long one, for less than half an hour had passed before Miss Elinora Todd emerged to board a brougham that had appeared, obviously by appointment.

We followed at a distance, just keeping the brougham in sight. It approached the church then turned away, whereupon we were obliged to draw nearer. Crossing several side-roads full of houses with long and blossom-filled front gardens, we emerged into a main thoroughfare lined by shops, a few inns and a livery stable. The brougham passed a warehouse building and began to lose speed. A few yards further on it came to a halt and Miss Elinora alighted. I handed the cabby his fee and stepped onto the pavement cautiously, anxious that Miss Elinora should be unaware of my presence.

I crossed the road with the intention of observing her reflection in a shop window as I had seen Holmes do on many occasions, but she did not walk far. Nearby was an Italian coffee shop called 'Callino's', with some of its seating spilling onto the pavement in the continental style. She approached a table where a man dressed in brown sat, and he immediately rose to seat her and order coffee for them both.

For I while, I observed their conversation, which appeared to be quite animated. Then, trusting in my disguise, I strolled with what I hoped was an unconcerned air back across the road. I saw to my relief that more of the tables were now occupied, and that one of those remaining was situated near where my quarry and her companion continued their discussion. I seated myself, and a waiter took my order of coffee and a slice of rich cake. I paid the bill immediately, since this would otherwise delay me should Miss Elinora leave suddenly.

This was, in fact, what happened some ten minutes later. The man in brown rose and paid the waiter who appeared, before holding the chair for Miss Elinora and leaving with her. They boarded a passing hansom, causing me some difficulty because I had no means to follow. I watched with my spirits sinking until they were almost out of sight, then a four-wheeler came to rest and four men alighted outside a tailor's shop. There was something about their demeanour that suggested to me that they were about to be dressed for a wedding, but I dismissed this irrelevant thought as I boarded and ordered the driver to proceed at all speed. This instruction was apparently not unusual to him, for he whipped up the horses without a word and we sped away. We quickly caught up with the hansom and, at my direction, adopted a slower pace. This man had clearly followed other vehicles before, since he at no time appeared surprised and conducted the pursuit largely without my further instructions. We eventually reached Tottenham Court Road, where the hansom turned into a narrow side-street.

I ordered the cabby to stop a few yards past the junction and, after dismissing him, hurried back to the side-street. I was in time to see Miss Elinora and her companion enter a nearby house as the hansom left. There seemed to be no sign of life in this small and silent street and so, feeling rather foolish, I stationed myself in concealment behind a thick bush in an opposite front garden. After little more than an hour, she emerged alone. Immediately, a hansom appeared from the direction of Tottenham Court Road, evidently by arrangement. She was then swept away, and this time I had no means to continue my pursuit. When she passed out of sight I walked until another hansom presented itself and was thus conveyed back to Baker Street, already hearing in my mind

Holmes' reproach at my failure to carry out the task that he had entrusted to me.

#

He laid aside his clay pipe as I entered. His expression told me that his day had gone well, and I was grateful.

"Ah, Watson," he beamed. "You have returned earlier than expected."

"I assume your case concluded satisfactorily?" I enquired, hoping to delay the inevitable.

He nodded, cheerfully. "The child is now safely at home and a cruel abductor is where he can do no more harm. But tell me, what of your day? I am anxious to hear your progress."

First I called for a pitcher of hot water and, ignoring Mrs Hudson's horror at my appearance, restored my normal self.

Holmes watched impatiently as I settled myself in an armchair with a glass of brandy. I then related to him all that I had observed and heard since the interlude at Callino's, as he sat silently listening with his chin upon steepled fingers.

"Did you overhear any of the conversation between Miss Elinora and the man who wore brown?" he asked when I had finished.

"I did, and I am at a loss to understand what hold this man has over her."

"Pray elaborate on what was said."

"It was strange talk, much like the planning of a military campaign. I listened, but could make nothing of it."

I saw from his eyes that this was not unexpected, but a possibility occurred to me.

"Holmes! Could it be that Miss Elinora, with her precise nature and mathematical skill, has devised some strategy for the government, and the man is their representative?"

The faintest of smiles crossed his features, and was quickly gone. "I think not, old friend."

"Then I can think of nothing more."

"Was there anything of significance about the appearance of this fellow?" He asked after a moment's silence.

"I noticed that he had a squint, probably of nervous origin."

"Was there anything more? Think, Watson!"

Seeing his increased interest, I searched my memory. "He had a pronounced limp, favouring his right leg."

"Capital!" Holmes looked positively elated. "You have done well, old fellow."

"Holmes, I was unable to follow Miss Elinora when she left the house off Tottenham Court Road. I can hardly claim any success."

"Much to the contrary," he held up his hands and smiled with satisfaction. "You have virtually solved the case."

"I confess to being confounded."

Holmes stretched his long body and stood up. "In ten minutes, if she follows her usual custom, Mrs Hudson will serve dinner. I recognise the aroma that has pervaded this room for some little while as that of curried chicken. Afterwards we will repair as usual to our chairs around that unlit fire and read or talk over our past experiences. Tomorrow morning we will visit Lestrade at the Yard and I will give him information which he will gratefully receive. But I perceive, Watson, that you are impatient to learn of the truth of this case and of my deductions. It was not a difficult problem and I will tell you all when we hear of its successful conclusion, but for now I will ask you one question – what is situated opposite Callino's, where you sat near Miss Elinora and Erdwell Cornish?"

"Who is Erdwell Cornish?"

"That is the real name, and the one known to Scotland Yard, of the man who wore brown."

I tried to remember my surroundings, as they had been while sitting at the coffee shop. Finally, it came to me. "The Landworkers and Stonemasons Bank!"

"Precisely," said Holmes, and would be drawn no further.

#

Inspector Lestrade did not sit down with us. He paced his office with the air of a man with a great weight on his shoulders.

"I hope you are not here for information and advice, Mr Holmes. I have little time to spare, since my investigation into this latest series of bank robberies is not going well. We have exhausted every line of enquiry, and discovered nothing."

"Which is why we are here," Holmes suppressed a grin. "If you would care to spare us a few moments, I am quite certain that I can provide you with the time and place of the gang's next appearance."

The Inspector ceased his pacing at once. "How could you have learned of this?"

“Oh, it was something that arose from a trifling affair that I was asked to look into. It often happens that way.”

“I admit to being desperate enough to listen to any theory. I am clutching at straws, and would welcome anything new.”

I could see that Holmes was enjoying the situation. He let a few moments pass before answering. Apprehension filled Lestrade’s face.

“I can tell you only this,” my friend said. “You will successfully conclude your case if you station six armed constables inside the Landworkers and Stonemasons Bank, in the late afternoon but before closing time tomorrow. I suggest that they enter the premises in plain clothes, in case the gang are observing the place.”

“How did you come by this information?” Lestrade asked in astonishment.

“As I said, Inspector, it was incidental. However, I do urge you to follow my instructions, and not to delay.”

To my surprise, Inspector Lestrade appeared unconvinced.

“Have you any other advice, Mr Holmes?” he said with a hint of sarcasm.

“I have, Lestrade. Do not be surprised if, in the course of this, you encounter Erdwell Cornish.”

“I would very much like to do so.”

“Act upon my instructions, and you will.”

#

The following day proved uneventful. I felt much stronger than of late, and telegraphed my locum to announce my intended return to my practice soon. Holmes spent much of the time bringing his index up to date, but there was an air of expectancy about him at all times. I could tell that his finely-tuned senses were constantly alert for a ring of the door-bell or the arrival of the telegram boy.

It was just after dinner when a message finally arrived. Mrs Hudson had no sooner cleared the plates away, than she re-entered our room bearing a telegram.

Holmes thanked her and tore open the envelope. The door closed behind her as he cast his eyes hurriedly over its contents.

"Capital!" he cried. "Lestrade wishes to see us at the Yard in the morning."

"I fear that I cannot attend, Holmes. I have already made plans to relieve my locum."

He hesitated for a moment, I like to think because I was unable to accompany him. "No matter, old fellow. I will relate all to you after dinner tomorrow."

I slept uneasily that night, my thoughts divided between anticipation of what my practice might hold and the fate of Mr Todd's sister. I hoped fervently that she had come to no harm at the hands of Erdwell Cornish and his gang. Try as I might, I could not form a clear picture of the part she had played in this affair, nor of what it was that Cornish apparently held over her head to gain from her some sort of complicity.

I breakfasted alone, Holmes having reverted to his usual habit of rising late. On arrival at my surgery I noticed that my locum had an air of impatience about him, like that of a runner awaiting the firing of the starting pistol. I soon discovered the reason, as he explained that an unseasonable local epidemic of bronchitis had kept him far busier than he was accustomed to. He left to return to his country practice with evident relief.

Throughout the morning I attended to a steady stream of patients. The time passed slowly, probably because I was anxious to hear from Holmes of Lestrade's account of the outcome of yesterday's events.

When at last I climbed the stairs to our rooms in Baker Street, it was to dark and mournful music. I recognised it as one of Holmes' own compositions, wrung from his Stradivarius with painstaking care.

"Watson!" Despite the tone of the music his mood appeared to be pleasant. I hung up my hat and coat as he put away his violin. "I have poured us both a glass of port."

Soon we were sitting opposite each other around the cold fireplace, having emptied our glasses.

"Mrs Hudson has said to expect dinner in half an hour," he informed me, "after which I am sure you would like me to relate to you my interview with Lestrade."

"That has not been far from my mind all day, so I would appreciate a description now. There is much that puzzles me still, Holmes."

"Very well," he said with a tone that indicated his disapproval of my impatience. "I will begin at the beginning, which is always simplest."

He sat back in his chair and I leaned forward eagerly in mine. "You have my entire attention."

After a quick look in my direction, he closed his eyes and began. "When I arrived at Scotland Yard earlier I knew instantly, from Lestrade's mood and the general atmosphere, that all had gone well the day before. He took great pride in explaining the strategy he employed, the result of which was the capture of the entire gang. There was but one casualty – Erdwell Cornish was foolish enough to draw a weapon when several police guns were trained upon him."

"He is dead?"

"Of necessity."

"What of Elinora Todd?"

"Let me tell the tale, Watson."

"But is she unharmed?"

"She is."

"I apologise, Holmes. Please continue."

He straightened his posture, his eyes open now. "At my request, and in consideration of the assistance he obtained from us, Lestrade allowed me to interview Miss Todd, who is now in custody. As a result, I now have a full understanding of the part she played in all this. It may come as a shock to you old fellow, when I say that I have seldom met such a scheming woman and hope never to do so again."

I felt my spirits plummet. "You astonish me."

"I first suspected that she was not all that she seemed, when Mr Todd took us to meet her. The way she managed the house, the pictures in the exact centre of the wall and everything in a clearly defined place told of a precisely attuned mind, admirable in itself, but her eyes and expression, her entire attitude, told more. Mr Todd attributed her ways to the loss of a suitor, and truly felt for her, when in fact they were symptoms of a burning jealousy of her brother's wealth and a strong hatred of the banks which, as she saw it, robbed her of her share of her father's estate.

"We will probably never have a true account of how she came to meet Trent, or Cornish as it turns out, for of that she would not speak. However, I consider it probable that she already had some sort of future plan in mind when she took up the study of mathematics before her father's death. Of course, when her brother later discovered her relationship with Trent and forbade her to continue, her jealous hatred was intensified."

"When we returned here, on the day we first met Mr Todd, I consulted my index because this fellow Trent had stirred something in my memory. I discovered that the name had been used by Cornish previously for a variety of crimes, and asked myself what his objective could be now. The most prominent recent criminal activity was the series of bank robberies that Lestrade was so worried about, and so I reviewed such information that I had. I found that they had taken place on the 8th of February, the 17th of March, the 9th of April and the 22nd of May, whereupon I realised at once that each date was two days after Miss Elinora had returned home after her short stays with 'Miss Heald'. Further enquiries revealed that five banks were involved in the ill-fated consortium in which Miss Elinora had invested, and four of these were the subjects of the previous robberies. I am sure, Watson, that you have already deduced the name of the fifth bank."

"The Landworkers and Stonemasons Bank, of course."

"Precisely. The meetings were actually with Trent, or Cornish, and were never of a romantic nature. She grew weary of excusing herself to her brother, hence the 'memory losses' which absolved her from inventing anything more. Mr Todd's insistence on medical help were a considerable inconvenience to her."

“But Holmes, what crime did she actually commit?”

He shook his head, with the air of someone explaining to a child. “Have you not realised yet? The study of mathematics, the precision upon which all her actions depended? She was the driving force, the planner of the whole series of crimes. Ample evidence of her guilt was found in Cornish’s rooms, off the Tottenham Court Road where you concluded your observations yesterday. You heard as much yourself when you sat listening in Callino’s.”

“I would never have imagined it,” I sighed. “Never.”

“You see, Watson, that my mistrust of the fair sex is not so unreasonable, after all.”

“She will doubtlessly share the fate of the rest of the gang.”

“They were, without exception, men who have spent their lives drifting from one crime to another. Men who are for hire when someone of a superior mind and criminal inclination sees a dishonest opportunity. But yes, she will share their fate and, I fear, be considerably older when she is again a free woman.”

We were silent for some time, before I remarked. “Sad as it will be, Holmes, we can now furnish an explanation to Mr Septimus Todd.”

He nodded slowly, and there was no cheer in his expression. “That is true, old friend, we will have given him an answer. But not, I am truly sorry to say, without breaking his heart in the process.”

The Adventure of the House Abandoned

In examining the contents of my dispatch box, temporarily retrieved from the vaults of Cox & Co., I have discovered my notes concerning a case that I had almost forgotten, and that I cannot remember my friend Mr Sherlock Holmes mentioning since its conclusion. However, since he has indicated no restriction on my placing the account before my readers, I now do so to the best of my recollection.

It was some little time after my friend had brought the affair that I have documented elsewhere as 'The Adventure of Marcus Davery' to its successful end that these events took place. Holmes was, for once, in an uncharacteristically light frame of mind because of the favourable development of several cases which he had watched closely. He had remarked that, although he was at present unoccupied, he had high hopes for the seeds he had sown in penetrating four impending criminal enterprises to bear fruit before long.

"It appears then, that you expect to be extremely busy in the weeks to come," I replied, lowering my morning edition of The Standard.

"I would consider that extremely likely. Adrian Tynan seeks to escape the rope after cruelly disposing of his mother-in-law, and that scoundrel Jake Meredith believes that his plans for robbing the mail train on the night of the forthcoming gold shipment are known only to himself and his lieutenants. Both, I think, will be disappointed. I have informed Lestrade as to my findings, and will accompany the official force at their capture. I would greatly appreciate your company on those occasions, Watson, if you are free."

I took out my pipe. "When you specify the dates, Holmes, I will make arrangements for my practice to be covered. As always, I will be pleased to be with you,"

"Excellent!" He leaned forward abruptly in his chair, listening. "But I do believe that Mrs Hudson is at the front door speaking in urgent tones to someone. It may be that we are to receive a new client."

I replaced my pipe unused in its pouch and stood up expectantly. A moment later we heard footsteps ascending the stairs, as well as those of our housekeeper which were familiar to us.

"A lady," my friend deduced from the tread, "and, from the tone of her voice, rather confused."

Mrs Hudson admitted a young lady of average height who I would have thought to be about twenty-five years of age. Her hair was very dark but her facial features, although not unattractive, struck me as rather sharp. I was sorry to see that she appeared to be in a highly nervous state.

"Miss Laura Willis to see you, Mr Holmes," our housekeeper announced, and was about to withdraw when Holmes called for tea.

"I must apologise for having no appointment," Miss Willis began in a muffled voice. "I hoped that you would see me regardless. It is kind of you to do so."

I saw at once that my friend's interest was aroused by her stiff movements and indistinct speech.

"But I see that you are ill. Come, be seated near the fire and rest yourself, and then tell us what brings you to us after you have taken tea." He paused until she was settled. "I am Sherlock

Holmes and this is my friend and colleague Doctor John Watson. You have my assurance that his discretion is equal to my own."

Mrs Hudson reappeared with the tea tray after a few minutes had passed and I poured for the three of us. I noticed that Holmes' eyes never left our client, as he studied her closely. We replaced our empty cups and she hesitated, then anxious words poured from her mouth before either of us could prompt her.

"Mr Holmes, I saw mention of you in a newspaper. Is it true that you investigate strange situations, such as are sometimes dismissed by the official police?"

"There have been many occasions of that sort, over the years," he replied. "Tell me, pray, is your reason for consulting me connected with the bruising that I now see as you turn your face to the light?"

For an instant, she dropped her gaze to the carpet. "It is directly connected."

"Who has treated you so?" said I, but Holmes dismissed my question with an impatient glance.

"Take a moment to consider," he advised, "and then tell us all at your leisure. There is no need to hurry."

Miss Willis nodded, her gaze taking in both of us in turn. "Thank you, gentlemen. The marks on my face and, indeed, on my body, are the result of a whipping I received at the hands of an unknown man. I do not know why he treated me so, nor am I aware of his identity, and that is why, in my confusion, I have sought your help."

"Any man who would treat a lady in this manner is an absolute scoundrel!" I retorted.

"Relate all that occurred, from the beginning, I beg of you." Holmes asked quietly.

"I am employed as a seamstress at Beales and Welford, of Lewisham," she said in a soft voice. "Three days ago I completed my work for the day and left the premises at six o'clock as is my usual practice. My lodgings are not far away, no more than a ten-minute walk, and I was about halfway there when I suddenly realised that I had been alone in the street since leaving the main thoroughfare, and that a man walked persistently behind me."

"Were you able to take note of his appearance?" Holmes enquired.

"As soon as I suspected his pursuit I glanced quickly behind me. I saw a man who was tall and thin with a short, pointed beard."

"Did he speak to you?"

"Not until later. A coach came to rest just ahead of me, and the man who followed quickly closed in. I felt his strong grip on my shoulder, and had no time to scream before a piece of cloth or muslin was pressed against my face. I can dimly recall a smell such as is present in hospitals or doctor's surgeries, before being carried into the coach."

"Chloroform," said I.

"Undoubtedly," Holmes agreed.

"I remember nothing more," our client resumed, "until I awoke in a well-furnished sitting-room. For an instant I believed myself to have fainted or been taken ill and brought there, perhaps while a doctor was summoned. I looked around me at the tasteful decorations and furniture, and suddenly realised that I was tied hand and foot to a stiff-backed chair."

“Were your abductors present, then?”

“Indeed they were, Mr Holmes, and they immediately began to question me. Repeatedly they shouted ‘Where is it?’ Or ‘What have you done with it?’ until I could stand it no more. I screamed at them, and shouted that I knew not to what they were referring, and that was when the whipping began.”

I felt a surge of outraged anger but said nothing. Holmes leaned towards her and spoke in his gentlest tone.

“I see that they have used you most cruelly. Did these men then specify what it was that they believed you to have hidden?”

“They did, but it meant nothing to me. I was accused of stealing documents, the plans of something called, ‘The Thunderer’.”

“And you are completely unaware of their meaning?”

“I swear that I have never heard such a title.”

Holmes closed his eyes briefly, in contemplation. “Pray continue, your narrative grows more interesting.”

“I was struck several more times, as you see. Then their assaults ceased suddenly when the second man, a short bald individual who I presumed to have driven the coach, left the room. The bearded man sat on the sofa drinking brandy, and I believe that I fainted.”

“That is not surprising.” I remarked.

She nodded. “I came to myself feeling weak and ill, just as the short man returned. He spoke quickly to the other and they both stared at me. I think they discussed whether to kill me, for some minutes. Then the bearded man shrugged and said that I could not harm them, and that I would probably starve to death before I was discovered. They did nothing more, but turned their backs on me and left. I saw nothing more of them."

"Do you know why they left so abruptly?"

"I cannot be certain, but the short man returned in a state of excitement. Possibly they had received urgent news that made their presence necessary elsewhere."

"That may be. How then, did you free yourself?" Holmes enquired.

"When I felt able, I do not know how much time had passed by then, I began to struggle against my bonds. At first it seemed hopeless, but after a while I came to realise that the chair was old and that some of its joints were loose. Although by now hungry and thirsty I redoubled my efforts and loosened them further, and it was by doing this that the chair turned around and I saw the short flight of steps leading down to another chamber. I moved the chair across the room and hesitated at the top of the steps, unwilling to suffer further injuries. Then, with no other course open to me, I tipped myself forward so that the chair was beneath me. The fall was of course painful and I screamed once more, even weeping as I came to rest at the bottom of the steps. When the pain had passed I thought that my efforts had been futile, until I found that the back of the chair had shattered and one of my arms was now free."

"I commend you on your endurance and bravery," Holmes said, and I concurred.

"Thank you, gentlemen, for listening to my experience and for your patience," she said with relief in her voice. "There is not much more to tell. I sat in one of the armchairs until my senses returned to me. I found some bread in the other room, which I discovered to be a kitchen, and drank some brandy from the decanter that the men had used. When I finally gained the strength to leave the house, I found to my amazement that I was no more than a few streets away from my lodgings! I forced myself to walk, my unsteadiness attracting many curious glances until I came upon Lewisham police station, where my account was received with some incredulity. I believe that the desk sergeant smelled the brandy on my breath, and rather than accept that it had been taken as a restorative, chose to believe that I had spent time in a tavern. But I persisted, and eventually a constable was despatched to accompany me back to the house. The street was composed of numerous shops, a small factory and many dwellings and, as I have said, was not far away. Inside the place of my confinement I was appalled to discover that the broken chair and the ropes that had bound me had disappeared, as had the decanter and all signs that the room had been inhabited. My first thought was that I had somehow brought the constable to the wrong house completely, but a moment of consideration told me that this could not possibly be, especially as the mirror near the entrance and the full-length portrait of a lady who could have been my sister were as I remembered."

"Do you, in fact, have such a sister?"

"Not at all. My only relative is an elderly uncle, who lives in Northumberland."

My friend nodded slowly. "And what did the constable make of this?"

Miss Willis' face reddened visibly. "He was most impolite. He made remarks to the effect that I should give up drinking if I could not hold my spirits. I think those were his words. He also swore rudely as he left."

"I am not surprised to hear it. Most of the official force are confounded at the first suggestion of the unusual, and shrink from it." He said nothing for a few moments, and then straightened his posture. "It is apparent then, that you have been mistaken for another person. The resemblance of the picture near the entrance to yourself reveals this immediately. Thus is explained your being held in an unfamiliar room where you were assumed to have hidden an item of which you have no knowledge. As to the nature of that item we have no means of identification, although I have a high expectancy of my investigation revealing it before long. Are you now quite recovered from your ordeal?"

"I returned to my lodgings yesterday afternoon, and slept long and heavily after consuming food and drink. When I awoke I felt sore, but sufficiently recovered to come here today."

"Capital! If you will give Doctor Watson the address of this house, we will pay a visit there after luncheon. Is there anything else you wish us to know of this?"

Miss Willis shook her head. "No, Mr Holmes, I think….but wait! I believe I failed to mention that my captors spoke with foreign accents."

"Thank you," Holmes said after a pause. "I had suspected that. If you will allow the good doctor to show you out, I think I can confidently say that you will hear from us quite soon."

#

After depositing Miss Willis in a cab, I climbed the stairs to our rooms with a question in my mind.

"Holmes, why do you suppose that the two men returned to the house, after Miss Willis had escaped?"

He looked up from the volume of his index that lay open on his lap.

"I imagine that they had reconsidered, and decided that to let her live was dangerous to them. On returning and finding her gone, they did what they could to erase all traces of the incident, making detection by the official force more difficult." He considered for a moment. "A possible alternative theory is that they observed Miss Willis leaving the house and, knowing that to attempt her murder in the street would probably attract the attention of passers-by at that time of day, they decided to remove what evidence they could to make the accuracy of her story seem unlikely."

"Who are these blackguards, Holmes?"

"I am not yet certain, but already I have my suspicions. Nevertheless, this afternoon our first action must be to visit that house ourselves, in the hope that the constable has not entirely destroyed all valuable indications by his blundering. I take it that you are with me?"

"As ever," I smiled.

"Capital! But I hear Mrs Hudson on the stairs, so doubtless lunch is imminent. The moment we have fortified ourselves sufficiently, we will set out on the trail of these men who ill-treat helpless women."

#

It was not yet mid-afternoon as we watched the hansom out of sight. We found ourselves in a street that was very much as Miss Willis had described, a long line of Georgian houses with many shops and a factory which manufactured replacement teeth.

"Is the place, Watson?"

I took out my notebook. "Miss Willis stated the address as 41, Ordmond Place. There is no number on the door, but counting from the nearby houses brings us to here. Also, the windows are dusty and the front garden has received no attention for some little time, and from our client's indications it seems obvious that the owner was absent."

A fleeting smile crossed my friend's face, and I could not tell whether it was in approval of my small deductions or as mockery of them. On reaching the front door he rapped upon it twice with his cane, before producing his pick-lock to gain admittance.

We stood in a carpeted hallway. There were no sounds. Holmes saw at once the picture that Miss Willis had described, hanging opposite a full-length mirror.

"There is indeed a close resemblance," he observed, "but no one with whom she was familiar would mistake Miss Willis for this lady."

"No, indeed," said I. "Her abductors may have acted upon a description by a third person, or perhaps they had a poor likeness to work from."

He nodded. "Both are possibilities. Now, let us examine this room and the kitchen, which I presume is behind that door ahead. The entire space is carpeted, which indicates that the owner, whoever she may be, is quite wealthy but also hampers my investigation. You have seen me reconstruct events from marks on a dusty floor, before now."

This was true, but not applicable here. Nevertheless, I stood against one wall while Holmes kneeled to examine the carpet through his lens. He eventually came upon the short flight of stairs that our client had described.

"Ha! If we needed substantiation of Miss Willis' account, Watson, we have it here. Her abductors clearly took considerable trouble to leave no trace, but these splinters from the shattered chair eluded them. Also, the tiny fragments of ash dropped upon the carpet are of a tobacco mixture not usually found in England, as I had come to expect. My studies that enabled me to write a monograph on the subject have not been in vain."

"Has the kitchen given up any clues?"

"Only the fact that there are fresh water traces in the pitcher. They did not taste stale, and the vessel was therefore used recently, probably to dilute the men's drinks. I think we have learned all we can here, however, so we will progress to the next stage of our enquiry."

"And what is that to be?"

He rose to his full height. "As we arrived, I noticed that we were under observation from the house opposite. A woman, I think, with long dark hair. If it is her habit to be so inquisitive, she may have seen something that can be useful to us."

We left the house shortly afterwards, re-locking it after Holmes had satisfied himself that all was as it had been on our arrival. After crossing the street we approached the residence that he had specified, a house almost identical to that we had just left with a tiny front garden beset with weeds. He rang the door-bell without response, and was about to rap upon the door with his cane when we heard faint footsteps from within. A moment later the door swung open, to reveal a tall thin woman with long dark hair. She wore a garment quite unlike usual female apparel, a long piece of cloth wrapped around her body somewhat resembling the Indian sari, but with the most intricate and fantastic designs along its length. The overall impression, I thought, was something like a gypsy fortune-teller at a travelling fair or circus.

She scrutinized us from beneath long eyelashes, her gaze passing from Holmes to me. Her slow smile encompassed us, and she spoke unhurriedly, in a husky, almost masculine voice.

"Forgive me gentlemen, for not answering your summons immediately. At this time of day I commune with the spirits, and one cannot leave that far-off plane hurriedly."

Holmes and I glanced at each other, trying to conceal our surprise.

"We apologise for disturbing you," my friend said with a straight face, "but we are anxious to speak to the occupant of the house opposite. It is a lady who lives alone, we are told."

A faint shadow of suspicion clouded her expression for a moment. "And who are you gentlemen, may I enquire?"

"My name is Sherlock Holmes, and this is my colleague, Doctor John Watson. We are here in connection with a private matter."

"Your names I have heard somewhere, but I cannot bring their significance to mind." Her eyes settled on us again, and her smile returned. "I am Tanith le Grande, a servant of departed spirits. What is it that I can tell you?"

"To begin with," Holmes said after a moment of hesitation, "we would like to know when she was last seen here. Her home is empty and shows no sign of recent habitation."

"Her home is a house abandoned. Miss Stayforth has not lived there for the past few weeks. I fear that she has passed to another realm."

"Why do you believe such a thing?" I asked.

Miss le Grande stared at me as if I had asked a preposterous question. "The spirits told me, of course."

Holmes ignored this. "Do you know of any recent activity in her house, since Miss Stayforth left?"

"Recently I saw two gentlemen visit the premises. With them was a woman who bore some resemblance to Miss Stayforth, probably a relative. She appeared to have difficulty with her movements, and it struck me that she was either unwell or drunk. Sometime later the men left without the woman. If she is no longer there then she must have left during the night, or while I spoke with the departed."

"And you are quite sure that Miss Stayforth is no longer alive?"

"Of course, though I cannot tell what has befallen her. No, we will not….." Her voice changed, suddenly becoming deeper still. Her eyes glazed, as if she peered into the far distance. "But yes, I am hearing their voices. They are telling me that you, Doctor Watson, will see her again. You alone will see her again!"

I gaped at her in surprise, startled as much by the risen note of her speech as by the content of it. "What is your meaning, Miss le Grande? Either Miss Stayforth has passed on, or she has not. How am I concerned with this?"

"You will shortly discover…." But the glazed look had faded, and her tone changed to its former level. She covered her eyes with her hands and I saw a great shudder pass through her body. "Gentlemen," she said breathlessly, "I must apologise most profusely. It is unusual for the spirits to come upon me in the presence of others, except during a séance, when we strive to seek them out. I regret that I must rest now, for I am near to exhaustion."

"If I can be of any assistance…"

"No, I will be restored if I have sufficient sleep to regain my strength. Goodbye, gentlemen."

She retreated, closing the door before we could say anything more. We turned away, and struck out in the direction of the end of the road.

"I noticed several hansoms passing here during our conversation," Holmes said. "We should have no trouble procuring one quickly."

"You surprised me, Holmes, with so little comment on Miss le Grande's apparent seizure."

He laughed harshly. "I cannot believe that you were deceived for an instant. That was a contrived performance to speed our departure and confuse us, nothing more."

"I can see that she would appear convincing, to a believer."

"I noticed immediately her reluctance to admit us, probably because the contraptions she uses to conduct her séances were not concealed at this time of day, or were dismantled. Also, the aroma of raw opium followed her as she came out to us which, I suspect, is the source of any genuine trances she may experience. As for her sudden seizure, it was no more than common play-acting. I find it difficult to see how you are to encounter Miss Tayforth if, as the spirits are supposed to have revealed to Miss le Grande, she has already passed away. Perhaps you, too, will have a vision. Watson."

"I am not quite as dismissive of the supernatural as you, Holmes. You will recall a strange incident which I wrote of as 'The Moonlit Shadow', which was never satisfactorily explained."

"Much can be imagined from tricks of light and shade, and the effect of an uncertain atmosphere in a strange place contributes to such an illusion."

“You are right, old fellow, I am sure.” I conceded after a moment of thought.

“That woman is a charlatan, but she at least confirmed some of Miss Willis’ account.”

“It is a strange name she has,” I observed.

“Not her real one, I’ll be bound, but another invention meant to support her manufactured aura of mystery. She shares it with the Phoenician goddess of the moon.”

A cab emerged from a side-street, and came to a halt as Holmes signalled with his stick.

“Back to Baker Street, then?”

“Not at all. I think we must seek an audience with Mycroft.”

#

Less than an hour later we found ourselves sitting in an anonymous waiting-room in Whitehall. We had listened to the closing of doors and echoing of footsteps in the corridor for too long, for Holmes was beginning to show signs of impatience. Then the door opened and the uniformed lackey who had met us on arrival and conducted us in here reappeared, to inform us that my friend’s brother was now able to spare us a little of his valuable time. We were escorted further into the building until a row of doors at the end of a silent passage confronted us. Our guide rapped upon the first of these, waited for permission to enter and announced us. He withdrew as we stepped into a thickly-carpeted chamber, wood panelled and rather dark. Mycroft rose to his feet behind a massive desk of oak.

"Sherlock, and Doctor Watson! A pleasant surprise indeed. Pray be seated, you will find the chairs to your left to be the most comfortable."

When we were settled he asked if we would like tea. We both thanked him but declined. He sat with his arms folded across his ample frame and studied us for a few moments. Then, his conclusions doubtlessly formed, he spoke in a quiet voice.

"I see that you are both perturbed about something. This will certainly be the reason for your presence here today." He scrutinized Holmes carefully, before allowing his gaze to fall upon me. He stared briefly at the blotting-pad before him, then his eyes met ours. "Very well then, how can I assist you gentlemen?"

"We are attempting to discover the whereabouts of a missing woman," Holmes began. "It is likely that she is pursued also by those who wish her harm. In addition, there is the possibility that these are foreign agents who seek to extract information from her and so, Mycroft, as I have no means of recognising such people, I am forced to request your help."

The elder Holmes had begun to frown as my friend spoke, and his expression deepened with every word.

"Have you been able to discover where this lady normally resides, Sherlock?"

"We have, and we have visited the house to little avail. The address is 41, Ordmond Place, Lewisham."

At this, Mycroft's face went blank. "No doubt," he said after a moment, "the lady in question is Miss Iris Stayforth."

I must have betrayed my surprise, but Holmes stared at his brother impassively.

"She is one of your people, then?"

"It is imperative that you divulge to me the identity of your client, if there is one. I must know who else is concerned with this."

Holmes reflected briefly, then must have concluded that there could be no harm in confiding in his brother, though complete confidentiality was his usual practice.

"The lady who approached me is Miss Laura Willis. She did so because she was abducted, taken to the address in Lewisham and mistreated, with the object of forcing her to give up plans of which she knows nothing."

"Plans for what, pray, and why did these foreigners choose Miss Willis?"

"She apparently resembles Miss Stayforth, who lives not far away. They were probably watching the area, and abducted the wrong woman."

Mycroft nodded. "If they were working from a photographic portrait, that is quite possible. The two women are not actually related?"

"Not at all. The resemblance is close, but far from identical."

"I see." Mycroft's eyes narrowed. "I would be grateful if you would explain how you became aware of this, since by your own implication, you have never seen Miss Stayforth."

A shadow of a smile crossed Holmes' face. "I have already disclosed that we have visited the house. A full-length portrait of the lady graces the hallway."

"Of course," the elder Holmes said. "And the plans that seem to be the cause of this? You were about to tell me, moments ago."

“Miss Willis mentioned a name. It was, as I recall, ‘The Thunderer’.”

Again there was a heavy silence. For what seemed like an age, no one spoke or moved. When Mycroft looked up again, his face was solemn.

“I am very glad that I can take for granted, the absolute discretion of you gentlemen.”

A bird flew past the single tall window, twittering alarmingly. When that momentary distraction had passed, Holmes said coldly:

“You can indeed, Mycroft. I had thought we had demonstrated that sufficiently on past occasions.”

“Of course, dear boy, of course. I was merely emphasising the importance of what I am about to tell you. At once you will realise the enormity of this affair.”

“Pray proceed.” Holmes and I leaned forward together.

Mycroft hesitated, and I formed the impression that the words to come were torn from his conscience. He struggled to overcome his reluctance, as if he feared to betray a trust.

“Your conclusion that foreign agents are involved is correct. For some time now, word has reached us from our people in Imperial Germany that a huge gun, a cannon with a range far exceeding any in use until now, has been invented, tested and constructed. There has also been persistent reports that, although not imminent, war may not be many years away.”

“’The Thunderer’,” I ventured.

“Indeed. You can imagine the devastating effect such a weapon would have, on opposing forces with field guns of a lesser range. Experience had taught us that German assurances of continued peace cannot be trusted, leaving us with no choice but to maintain the development of our arms at least to a standard equal with theirs. To this end were arrangements made for a considerable sum to be paid to someone closely concerned with the design of this gun, in exchange for a duplicate set of plans. Our agent charged with the task of bringing them to London was unfortunately discovered and pursued into the capital. Realising this, she hid the documents, or at least that is what we believe."

"Our agent being Iris Stayforth," Holmes concluded.

"Indeed. She is highly skilled in the art of deception. In Germany she became the confidante of a high official in the Imperial court. Naturally, with foreign spies in such close pursuit, on her return to England she could not present herself at Whitehall or at any connected government department. We know that she arrived at her home, but she has since disappeared."

"But surely, it is unlikely that German agents disposed of her, since they would not do so until the hiding-place was revealed. Also, in that event the abduction of Miss Willis would never have taken place, much less her torture."

"Quite so, Sherlock. The only explanation is that she has met with some sort of accident, an event unknown to us, or more likely that Count von Schell has caught up with her."

"What part does he play in this?" my friend asked.

"He is the official I mentioned, who Miss Stayforth found it necessary to become close to in the course of her work. Of course she was known by a German name and had succeeded in falsely establishing herself as a member of an old Prussian family. As I said, she was a highly skilled agent. Apparently the Count had great affection for her and proposed marriage on several occasions. Finally, because at that time she was very near to obtaining the plans and it was imperative that her position was maintained, she agreed. Later, when her true purpose became known, Count von Schell swore that he would cause her to be hunted down and killed, to avenge the slur on his family name, as he put it. I fear that the man does not take disappointment well."

"So there is more than one hostile agency concerned here." Said I.

Mycroft shrugged. "Not necessarily. If the Count's people have murdered Miss Stayforth, they will have returned to Germany, for they have no interest in the plans. He is said to be a young man of impulsive and erratic nature so, even if aware of the situation regarding them, he would spare it no consideration."

"If they have done so," Holmes observed, "the other group do not know of it. Hence their mistakenly turning their intentions to Miss Willis."

"The indications are that they are working independently and unbeknown to each other."

Holmes spent a few minutes in contemplation, his head upon his chest. I was about to turn to him to speak, when he looked directly at his brother expectantly.

"You have identified one possibility that explains Miss Stayforth's disappearance, Mycroft. Are you now prepared to tell us the name of the two German agents who abducted Miss Willis?"

Again the elder Holmes was hesitant, and I reflected that he must be fighting an inner battle against the habit and official restrictions of a lifetime.

"To the best of our knowledge until now, there are but two German spies of any note working in the capital. One of those has been arrested and is currently being investigated concerning a different matter. So we are left with Herman Baumann, a contemporary of Oberstein, who you may remember has crossed your path and mine in the past. Baumann is thought to be a ruthless and intelligent man, obsessed, as his masters are, with the concept of his country eventually ruling all of Europe. While I consider that to be unrealistically ambitious, it does not bode well for the years to come. Should you chance to discover the plans in the course of your enquiries, Sherlock, you will of course convey them to me immediately?"

Holmes nodded. "Your trust in us is not misplaced, Mycroft. Pray be good enough to tell us where Baumann is to be found."

"He is in the habit of changing his place of residence often," Mycroft said, "probably because he suspects that he is being watched, which he is. I think, gentlemen, that sooner or later he will return to Ordmond Place, since the plans still have not been discovered. Your best course of action may be to lie in wait for him there."

#

We returned to Baker Street in time for a cigar before dinner. The conversation during the meal was interrupted by frequent silences, and I knew that this was because Holmes was considering how to proceed.

"We will return to Ordmond Place when it is fully dark, Watson," he said as he pushed away his plate. There are but two remaining problems. First we must devise a way to induce Baumann to join us tonight – we clearly cannot conduct a vigil indefinitely, awaiting his convenience – then we must ourselves attempt to discover the hiding-place of the plans. Knowing how long Miss Stayforth spent in her home before departing once more would be of immense assistance, but such information is not available to us."

“Such a pity. If we could make it appear that the plans are in danger of being lost or destroyed, perhaps it would attract Baumann quickly.”

Holmes smiled briefly. “Sometimes I could believe that it is you who can read my mind, Watson. I have already begun such a course of action, but I am doubtful if it will take effect tonight. That is why I mentioned two remaining problems.”

“You refer, I think, to the telegram you despatched, during our return from Whitehall.”

“Indeed. I wired Fleet Street, hoping for an insertion in the late editions. If this is in time to be seen by Baumann, we can be sure of his company tonight.”

“What was the message?” I enquired.

“Simply that the owners of 41, Ordmond Place (for Miss Stayforth is merely a tenant) have discovered instability in the foundations. They have therefore resolved to commit the place to demolition, without delay.”

“That would certainly attract Baumann’s immediate attention,” I agreed, “and the severe disapproval of the owners. This will cause them considerable difficulty, if they wish to re-let in the event of her not returning.”

He waved away my objection. “I will of course publish a retraction.”

#

Darkness had fallen some time earlier. Holmes and I watched the lights of the departing hansom grow fainter, and finally disappear.

“Ordmond Place is quiet tonight,” Holmes observed. “I will enter number 41 alone, Watson, while you conceal yourself among these bushes. Although they form the boundary of a garden, you should not be disturbed, since there are no lights showing in any windows hereabouts. You are armed, of course?"

"My service revolver is loaded and in my pocket."

"Capital! Remain concealed until you observe someone else entering, then follow with your weapon drawn. If our trap is not sprung in two hours or so, we may assume that Baumann has not seen the newspapers, or else he has not been deceived."

And so he entered and my vigil began. I crouched uncomfortably, with my face rubbing against twigs and leaves which rustled as a faint breeze sprang up. After a while a landau appeared, and deposited its passengers much further along the street. Two hansoms came and went in succession, and a solitary man, unsteady on his feet, ambled by from the other direction.

Just as I began to feel cramped, a four-wheeler arrived and two men alighted. I heard harsh remarks in guttural German as the conveyance left and the smaller of the two set off away from the house. The other man, in a cape and top hat, stood listening for some little time before, apparently satisfied that he was unobserved, advanced towards number 14 and picked the lock as Holmes had done. The door closed behind him softly.

I waited for no more than a minute or two, before rising with some relief and feeling the reassuring weight of my revolver in my hand. As I crossed the street I ensured that I was alone, and resolved to wait near the entrance until Baumann, if it was he, reappeared. He would then be confronted by me while Holmes stood guard at his back. Nevertheless, it seemed prudent to ascertain whether the door had been re-locked, and to my surprise it had not. I entered stealthily, momentarily startled by my reflection in the mirror in the hallway.

I saw a faint light ahead, and as I advanced a solitary oil lamp became visible near the hearth.

"You know me then?" Holmes said to the man whose question I had not heard, and who now held him at gunpoint.

"Oh yes, Mr Holmes," came the thickly-accented reply. "Our communications here are excellent. We are aware of your prowess at detection, and so it is most fortuitous that I should find you here, for who else is more capable at finding something that is lost? I would be obliged if you would conduct a search of this room and, if necessary, the others, until the missing document is discovered. I am aware also that you know of its contents, or else you would not be here, so you will have realised its importance to my country from which it was stolen."

"What has happened to the lady who lives here?" Holmes asked.

"Ah, a most intriguing woman, I am told. I had orders to dispose of her after she relinquished the document to me, but news has reached me that she has been dealt with elsewhere. This leaves me in a difficult position but I have every confidence that you will discover its hiding-place, sparing me the effort. You will begin searching at once."

I stood in the shadows. Holmes' adversary appeared formidable. His iron-grey moustache and whiskers seemed to bristle as he spoke, and his voice held the authority of the parade-ground. My friend had not moved, as I stepped forward with my weapon levelled.

"Good evening, Herr Baumann."

He whipped round to face me, enabling Holmes to grip him from behind and wrest the gun from his fingers.

"Who are you, sir? What right do you have here?"

"At least as much as you, I think." I answered.

"Excellent, Watson," said my friend. "Now all that remains is to convey this beauty to the official force, before we set about our own search."

"I suggest you begin at once. Let go your weapons go and unhand my comrade."

We all turned at this new voice, to see the indistinct figure of the other man I had seen earlier. I realised then, the terrible mistake I had made. This man had acted as a look-out, until he was certain that Baumann would be undisturbed. That was why he had left his comrade on arrival, to position himself nearby. It was for his return that the door had been left unlocked, enabling me to enter before him. He was the second man that Miss Willis had described. Inwardly I sighed, because I felt I had failed Holmes. Our discarded revolvers struck the carpet with a muffled impact.

"A timely entrance, Gruber." Baumann said in relieved tone. "If you will begin, Mr Holmes, we have not much time."

Holmes moved towards a cabinet where an assortment of porcelain was displayed. He paused and took out his pocket watch.

"Take care, Mr Holmes," warned Gruber, made wary by the gesture as he walked into the light.

"If you would be so good as to hurry," Baumann pointed to the cabinet with his retrieved gun.

My friend seemed to pause in his search, every few moments, and I formed the impression that he listened for some new sound.

He slammed a drawer noisily as if in impatience, but I realised that this was a signal as it was immediately followed by a rushing of heavy footfalls and three figures emerged from the gloom.

"It seems you were right, Mr Holmes," said Lestrade from near the door. "All right you two, these constables and I have you in our sights. Drop your pistols to the floor at once."

Baumann complied, but Gruber raised his weapon.

"Nein!" Baumann slapped his comrade's hand and the gun went spinning across the room.

"That was very sensible," said the inspector. He turned to the tallest constable. "Put the cuffs on them, Charlesworth,"

Baumann mumbled something in German, probably curses or regrets. Holmes smiled briefly as they were led away.

"I will see you at Scotland Yard in the morning, Lestrade," my friend assured the inspector.

"Evidently you telegraphed Scotland Yard, in addition to Fleet Street," I remarked when we were again alone.

"It seemed an appropriate precaution. Lestrade was to come here if he had not heard from me by ten o'clock."

"Are we to leave the finding of the plans to the official force, then? Or perhaps to your brother's people?"

"Very much to the contrary, Watson. I had deduced the hiding-place before Baumann's arrival, and the plans will be on Mycroft's desk before we visit Lestrade in the morning."

He approached a tall bookcase and pulled out a volume. Within it was a flat bundle of paper, secured by string.

"But how did you know which book concealed it, even if you identified the hiding-place?"

Holmes placed the papers in his pocket. "It was a simple observation, depending at first on the length of time that Miss Stayforth spent in this house before fleeing the agents of Count von Schell, who she knew were closing in. Obviously, the less time she had, the less intricate the place of concealment would be, and I quickly noticed the disturbance to the fine layer of dust that had accumulated on these bookshelves in her absence. Thus the particular book she had chosen was evident, and an attempt to remove it from between its companions proved difficult because of its increased thickness after the insertion of the plans. As soon as I became aware of Baumann's presence, I wiped away the dust with the sleeve of my coat so as to leave no indication, and began the search he ordered elsewhere. It really was quite uncomplicated, old fellow."

He made to leave, and I turned down the wick of the oil lamp and followed in the darkness. As I neared the door I became very still, because I had seen something for a fleeting instant that took away my breath and made movement impossible.

There before me stood a young woman, she of the picture on the nearby wall. She raised a hand in greeting and smiled, and my heart raced as I realised that she was as transparent as glass, Holmes being clearly visible beyond her. Almost immediately she faded from my sight, but I recalled at once the prediction of Tanith le Grande, that my friend had been so contemptuous of.

I felt a cold chill envelop me, though the image, or apparition, had not appeared hostile. Holmes paused in his departure and turned to look back at me, no doubt warned by the strange sense he sometimes displays when there is sudden alteration in my emotional state. I realised that he had seen the alarm in my face, and drawn his conclusions at once.

"It was the reflection of the picture in the mirror, nothing more," he assured me. "A glass of port on our return to Baker Street will steady your nerves."

I told myself that he was undoubtedly correct. That Tanith le Grande was a charlatan, like all those who made use of the supposed supernatural for their own profit. Holmes was usually right, in most things.

But I have never been sure.

"Do finish your tea, my dear Lestrade, and then having dispensed with trivialities, you can explain to Doctor Watson and myself the reason for this sudden and most unexpected visit this afternoon."

Sherlock Holmes leaned his thin body back in the armchair and waited. I put down my own cup, curious as to what the inspector had to tell us.

"Well, gentlemen," the little detective began, "the fact is that one of our own men has disappeared. It's been a week now, and he's not been back to The Yard, nor has anyone heard from him."

"An inspector?" asked Holmes.

"Indeed."

"His name, pray?"

"Northbridge, one of the most recent additions to the Detective Division."

My friend nodded slowly. "I know him by sight."

"We have of course made exhaustive efforts to discover his whereabouts, and some of us have continued in our own time, but our superiors have called us off officially because of the mounting pile of cases that await our attention. 1888 has been an exceptionally busy year for us, and we are only at the beginning of Summer."

"I understand your predicament, Inspector. I am aware that the demands on you and your colleagues has been especially heavy of late. Fortunately I have no current case, and so may be able to offer some assistance."

Lestrade, who did indeed appear as a man very hard-pressed, was visibly relieved.

"It would be helpful, perhaps, to know the nature of Inspector Northbridge's work at the time of his disappearance," I ventured to suggest.

"Excellent, Watson," said Holmes. "That is what I was about to ask. It would seem to be a good starting point."

The inspector hesitated, as was natural at the prospect of divulging Scotland Yard's business or intentions to outsiders, before informing us: "Northbridge was conducting an investigation into two particularly vicious murders, both committed within the last six weeks and thought to be connected since the method of dispatch was identical. I doubt if he got far with his enquiries, since he had been on the case only five days when we last heard from him."

"What was the method of dispatch?"

"Strangulation of the most brutal kind. The heads were half-severed from the bodies and the marks from the chain, or whatever it was, were distinctive."

Holmes stared thoughtfully at our sitting room ceiling. Suddenly, he got to his feet, strode over to the window and looked down on Baker Street with a pensive air.

"I think it best if we now accompany you to Scotland Yard, Inspector," said he. "If you would be so good as to allow me to see the file on your colleague and any other information that you may have there. Watson, if you would inform Mrs Hudson that we will not be in for lunch, I will retrieve our coats from the hat-stand."

Reluctantly, I passed the message to our landlady. Five minutes later we were seated in a hansom that passed our door conveniently as we emerged into the street.

When we were settled in Lestrade's cramped office, a constable was sent to fetch Inspector Northbridge's file. He was back in minutes, and I saw at once that something was amiss. He placed the file upon the desk and addressed Lestrade.

"Inspector…"

"What is it, Faring?"

The young man's expression deepened. "Sir, news has just reached us. The constable who has been checking Inspector Northbridge's house every day found the front door open and a body inside."

We all looked up, and it was Lestrade who spoke first. "Northbridge?"

"His mother, sir."

"Murdered?"

"Strangled, it appears. She had been dead for some hours."

The Inspector gave a despairing shake of his head. "All right. You can go, Faring."

We could still hear the young constable's retreating footsteps growing fainter along the corridor, as Lestrade spoke again: "I must go there at once."

'One moment, Lestrade. Am I to understand that Inspector Northbridge was a bachelor, living alone but for his mother?"

"That is correct, Mr Holmes. His father died some years ago."

“Very well. If you have no objection, Doctor Watson and I will accompany you.”

We arrived at the Finsbury house a short time later. The two constables on guard recognised Lestrade at once and stepped aside for us to enter. The little detective examined the elderly lady’s body with a single comment : “the same as the others”, but appeared to glean little else from the scene. Finally, he stood aside thoughtfully, gesturing that my friend could now apply his methods.

Holmes spent twenty minutes conducting his inspection, entering a room across the corridor briefly. Afterwards he looked around once more before coming to stand beside us near the door.

“Well, Mr Holmes, do you agree that the murderer has left little that can be of help?”

“Certainly his approach is that of a professional. However, we can be sure that he entered by the same door as ourselves, since there is the faint impression upon the mat of a fresh boot-mark pointing inwards. Also, as you yourself observed, the marks on the neck of the deceased and the severity of the wound agree with those of the two previous victims. He was evidently admitted willingly, since there are no signs of a struggle. There are any number of deceptions he could have used, to achieve this.”

Lestrade nodded. “Undoubtedly. Have you reached any other conclusions?”

“As you may have noticed, I left to make a quick examination of Northbridge’s bedroom. All is in order there, his clothes tidily arranged in a wardrobe and the floor clean.” Holmes handed Lestrade an engraved visiting card. “This may be of some significance. I retrieved it from where it had fallen, behind a bedside table in a corner.”

"Mr Godfrey Redstrap, Assistant Governor of the Agricultural & Landowners Bank." The Inspector read aloud.

"Indeed. With your permission we will accompany you again, since you will undoubtedly wish to interview Mr Redstrap this afternoon. I fear that Doctor Watson and myself would experience considerable difficulty were we to undertake this alone, since we are not attached to the official force."

#

Holmes said little over luncheon. I devoured Mrs Hudson's chicken pie with relish, while he ate little.

"Clearly, you have thought more of this," I observed from his expression. "Would you care to share your conclusions?"

Holmes put down his fork. "I am asking myself why a professional killer would take the life of the elderly mother of a missing police officer. There is no profit in it for him, and so it can only be to ensure her silence. As to what she knew that was perceived as threatening, that most likely was something told to her by her son, Inspector Northbridge. Possibly he has been murdered or kept prisoner for coming into possession of the same knowledge. Perhaps our interview with Mr Godfrey Redstrap will throw some light on this. We will meet Lestrade at the bank, which is a short distance from the mother of all banks in Threadneedle Street, in half an hour, so finish your lunch, Watson, and we will see what we can learn."

Soon after, we encountered the Scotland Yard detective on the steps of the Agricultural & Landowners Bank.

"I made the appointment with some difficulty," Lestrade said. "The importance of Mr Redstrap's position was impressed upon me, as was the fact that he is always extremely busy. Be that as it may, I will not let it stand in the way of my investigation into a murder, nor of discovering the whereabouts of a missing officer."

We were shown into a spacious chamber dominated by a huge, well-polished desk. Around the walls hung pictures of stern-looking men who I presumed were past holders of positions of high standing in the bank. Behind the desk, thick curtains hung around a single, tall window.

The man who rose to meet us was of impressive girth, florid-faced and quickly demonstrated an off-hand manner. He ignored Holmes and myself, and addressed Lestrade directly.

"You are an inspector from Scotland Yard, I am told." He said when we were seated.

"That is correct, sir."

"And what is it that brings you to me?"

"I understand that you were recently visited by my colleague, Inspector Northbridge."

"I cannot recall such an occasion."

Lestrade produced the card from his pocket. "This was found at his house. I assume that they are not given out indiscriminately."

Mr Redstrap's contemptuous look vanished, and his manner changed abruptly. He withdrew a large handkerchief from his waistcoat pocket and mopped his moist face.

'Ah, yes," he said haltingly, "it comes back to me now. It was about nine days ago. I was busy at the time, but I spared him a few minutes."

'Perhaps you could tell us of the nature of the interview?" Holmes asked.

Mr Redstrap glared at my friend for a long moment. "And who are you, sir?"

"My name is Sherlock Holmes."

Some of the banker's previous manner returned. "Indeed? I have heard of you. The consultant detective, are you not? You have no official authority, and no right to be here. I will summon a clerk to show you and your companion from the premises."

"Mr Holmes' presence is essential to my investigation," Lestrade broke in, "and I would very much appreciate your answer to his question."

The handkerchief was retrieved from where Mr Redstrap had dropped it on his desk. He wiped his perspiring face thoroughly, appearing increasingly nervous.

"The discussion was of a private nature."

Holmes fixed him with a cold glance. "The outcome may well have cost Inspector Northbridge his life."

"How can that be?"

"Northbridge has been missing for the last week," Lestrade explained. "We feel that it is possible that whatever he learned here caused him to pursue a course of action that resulted in his death."

"No, that cannot be so." Mr Redstrap's face grew noticeably paler. "As I remember, he asked about aspects of the Bank's security which, of course, are highly confidential. He mentioned that his enquiries had led him to believe that we are in some way at risk, but I was able to reassure him."

"So there was no truth in his suspicions?"

"None whatsoever."

"And nothing else was discussed?"

"Nothing."

The little detective looked across at Holmes. "Is there anything that you or Doctor Watson would like to add?"

"Nothing comes to mind," said I, breaking my silence.

"I think that we have learned all that is necessary," Holmes said.

We rose and left Mr Redstrap standing by his desk, evidently much relieved. No word was spoken until we reached the street.

"That man is definitely keeping something from us." Lestrade said when we had walked a short distance.

"Without a doubt," My friend paused before hailing a hansom. "Would it suit you, Lestrade, for us to continue this investigation into Inspector Northbridge's disappearance as you requested, while you return to The Yard to deal with his mother's murder and your accumulated cases? I promise to let you know if anything significant comes to light." Before a reply could be forthcoming, my friend raised his hand to attract a passing four-wheeler. As we boarded, he turned to the Scotland Yard man with some parting words. "Despite Mr Redstrap's assurances it would be as well, I think, to have some sort of watch kept on the bank. His lack of sincerity was obvious. Goodbye, Lestrade."

The coach bore us away swiftly, leaving the inspector standing on the pavement.

"Your expression tells me that you have questions, Watson," my friend said as the horses slowed their pace to round a corner.

"Doubtlessly, you have learned something that I missed."

"You cannot have failed to observe Mr Redstrap's anxiety, and his constant glances at the photographic portrait on his desk?"

"It was of a young girl of about fourteen years of age, inscribed 'Martha', and was taken at St Alvias Convent School."

"Precisely. Judging by her age and the resemblance, it would be difficult not to conclude that she is his daughter."

I nodded. "That was my conclusion, also."

"Then why do you think he repeatedly looked so fearfully at her portrait?"

"Perhaps because she is ill."

"I think not."

"But how can you tell?"

"There are many kinds of dread, Watson, that settle upon a man's countenance for various reasons. I am accustomed to some of them."

"Could it be, then, that she is in danger of some sort?"

"Bravo, Watson! From Mr Redstrap's secretive manner, I believe that she has been kidnapped and held hostage."

"That would certainly explain his behaviour."

"And his reluctance to speak, if he has been threatened."

"This seems likely, Holmes, but what has it to do with the disappearance of Inspector Northbridge?"

"That is what we must now endeavour to discover."

#

We arrived at our lodgings soon after, having stopped once at a Post Office. To my surprise, Holmes waited in the street while I went up to our rooms. He offered no explanation, but by looking from our window I quickly realised his intention.

"Did you find someone to take a message to the Irregulars?" I asked as he came in and took off his coat.

"I did indeed," he replied, smiling because I had correctly deduced his reason for accosting a young urchin. "That young fellow is a chimney sweep, but I have seen him before in the company of Wiggins."

"What service then, do you require from Wiggins and his friends?"

"The whereabouts of Hendon Warrilow's lodgings will do, for now."

"Who is Warrilow?" I asked.

"A well-known London criminal. Strangling is one of his specialities."

"You suspect that this man is involved in the murder of Inspector Northbridge's mother?"

"I consider it a distinct possibility. The marks on the lady's neck are indeed similar, and not only to the previous victims that Lestrade spoke of. I recall that they featured in a case of some three years ago, when Warrilow was suspected but released because the evidence against him was insufficient. I was not concerned in that affair, but it is noted in my index."

"I nodded. We wait then, to hear from the Irregulars?"

“For now. It is almost time for dinner, as you no doubt have observed. Afterwards it should not be long before a reply to my telegram is forthcoming.”

In fact it was after we had eaten, as we settled ourselves with the first pipe of the evening, when the telegram boy rang the door-bell. Holmes was on his feet in a flash, and downstairs before Mrs Hudson could emerge from the kitchen. He resumed his seat in a rush, tearing open the yellow envelope with his briar gripped between his teeth.

“As I suspected.” He nodded as he discarded the form. “Miss Martha Redstrap has not attended St Alvias Convent School for two weeks. The reason given was a mild attack of influenza. I cannot imagine this causing her father the anxiety that he was clearly suffering today. My theory, I think, is vindicated.”

Before I could reply, the door-bell rang again. My friend ceased knocking out the ash from his pipe at once, reaching the top of the stairs and raising a hand to once more preclude our landlady’s appearance. He was back in moments, with the air of a huntsman about him.

“Wiggins has not disappointed us!” he cried. “Our quarry resides at 85, Hyacinth Lane, which, as I recall, is just off the Tottenham Court Road. Come, Watson, we have a night’s work ahead of us.”

#

Holmes directed the driver to stop near a cluster of ancient oaks on the Tottenham Court Road. He surrendered the fare and we waited until the hansom was out of sight.

“Hyancinth Lane is about a hundred yards ahead,” he said, “just past that newly-painted fence.”

I could barely see the fence as we had walked some distance from the nearest street lamp, and few of the houses showed any illumination. I took out my pocket watch and held it near my face. It was after eleven.

"In here, Watson." We stepped into the lane and moved cautiously in the deepening darkness. After about five minutes, we passed several buildings lying back from the edge of the lane. The only sounds were from the shifting of the horses in the nearby stables, and the cry of a disturbed night-bird somewhere in the trees.

"I would not have expected a man such as Warrilow to live here," I whispered. "These houses seem far too grand."

Holmes said nothing, but pointed in the darkness. Because of the whiteness of his shirt-cuff, I was able to see which direction he indicated. The black shapes of two or three more houses, older and dilapidated I saw as we drew nearer, loomed ahead of us. As with the others, no rooms were illuminated. The furthest proved to be number 85, where we peered through the windows and listened at the door to no avail.

"That narrow passage will lead us to the back of the house," Holmes said quietly and led the way, making no sound.

"The occupiers are probably in their beds by now," I remarked unnecessarily.

"But I would expect Warrilow to be at his trade at any time of day or night. For him, this would not be an unreasonable hour."

The end of the passage held nothing new for us. The rear of the house too, had the look of a place abandoned. Holmes inspected the door as he had the front entrance, bending to get a closer view of something stuck to the stone step.

“Warrilow, or someone else, has been here quite recently,” he murmured. “This lump of earth from the sole of a boot is quite moist, having had insufficient time to dry. We will return to Baker Street now, I think, and return here a little earlier tomorrow.”

We were fortunate in returning to Tottenham Court Road as a hansom delivered a fare to one of the well-spaced houses along the thoroughfare. The weary driver took us to our lodgings quickly, talking encouragingly to his horse. Once inside our rooms, Holmes bade me goodnight and retired immediately. I smoked a lonely pipe before doing the same.

The next day proved largely uneventful. I attended my practiced briefly to ensure that my locum was coping with my increasing number of patients. On my return in the afternoon I noticed a pad of telegram forms, discarded carelessly on the dining-table. Holmes lounged lazily in his armchair.

‘I see that you are wondering as to my actions in your absence,” he said in a tired voice. “Lestrade had informed me that the names of the previous two victims of Warrilow, if indeed it was he who murdered them, are Frederick Purcell and Stephen Mortimer. He neglected to mention their professions and it occurred to me that they may be significant. I think we can expect his answer, soon after dinner.”

But for once my friend was in error. No telegram had arrived by nine o’clock when we again set out for Warrilow’s house.

#

Again we directed the driver of the hansom to stop on the Tottenham Court Road. The fellow was slow in complying, and so we were about to alight at a place nearer to the junction with Hyacinth Lane.

“Wait!” Holmes exclaimed suddenly.

I stopped, with one foot on the pavement, and turned to him in surprise. A cart, pulled by a coal-black horse, had emerged at a gallop from Hyacinth Lane and was speeding away in the direction from which we had come.

"Driver!" My friend called up through the little trap-door. "An extra sovereign to your fare if you turn and follow that cart at a distance. On no account must you be seen to be in pursuit."

The man's muffled response came as he turned the hansom and set the horse to a trot.

"Was that Warrilow?" I asked.

"I am quite sure of it," Holmes confirmed, "despite the darkness. He passed beneath a street-lamp and a glimpse sufficed for me to recognise him."

"Would it not have been better to enter his house while he is away, in order to see if anything that could be helpful to our investigation is there, rather than follow him without knowing his destination?"

In the poor light, I fancied that I saw Holmes smile. "Wherever Warrilow is bound for, you can be sure that he is up to no good. It may be that he is meeting other members of a gang that he is connected to, or that he is on his way to claim another victim for reasons we do not yet know. In any event, I intend to choose my moment to confront and question him."

We said nothing for a while, as the horse plodded on before us keeping the cart in sight. Now and then other hansoms and an occasional landau or four-wheeler appeared, to turn off again within a mile or two. One of these remained on the road, between us and the cart we pursued. For much of the journey, it helped to conceal us.

“We are entering Hammersmith,” said I presently, breaking the silence.

Holmes lifted his head from his chest. “Indeed. Where, I wonder, is Warrilow taking us.”

We were soon to find out, for the cart took two turns to the left then three to the right, finally coming to rest before one of a group of villas that stood behind well-kept lawns. The street lamps here were bright enough for us to see Warrilow alight and tether his horse to a lamp-post as we passed.

The road curved, and the driver halted the hansom as soon as we were out of sight of the house. Holmes told him to wait, and we walked back without speaking. We arrived as Warrilow was admitted by an elderly butler. Holmes held a finger to his lips to indicate that I should remain silent, and we turned onto the path that led to the front door. I think that my friend’s intention was to gain entrance at the back of the house, but he came to a sudden halt as light flared in the front room. The glow increased and he motioned me to follow as he crawled silently beneath the big bay window, where a fanlight had been opened to let in the warm night air.

We settled ourselves, I cannot say comfortably, and strained our ears.

“You cannot do this!” said a voice that I recognised. “You scoundrel, sir! How dare you keep her from me!”

“It is in your own hands,” another voice replied, and Holmes mouthed the word ‘Warrilow’ by way of identification.

“I would be betraying years of trust. It would ruin me,” The first voice, that of Mr Redstrap, the bank official, complained despairingly.

“It is either that, or your daughter’s life. The choice is yours. We have said these things before now, let us not waste time doing so again.”

There was a long silence then, and a murmuring of words that we were unable to hear.

Finally, Mr Redstrapp exploded in a burst of anger. “Take it then, and may you go to hell! When will I see my daughter?”

“This very night. I will send her to you in a hansom.”

The thud of heavy footsteps reached us as Warrilow left the house and we took shelter behind a bush as he walked quickly down the path to the road. From within the house I heard the sound of someone crying softly.

When the cart disappeared from our sight we ran back to the hansom. The driver had apparently anticipated our needs and turned his vehicle around.

“Pray continue to follow that cart,” Holmes instructed him, and the horse surged forward.

He said no more, but watched the road before us constantly. After a while the cart turned into a maze of dark side-streets and our driver had to proceed more slowly, lest our pursuit be discovered. We entered a long road with terraced houses along one side, while the other boasted buildings that appeared to be warehouses. Warrilow had disappeared but this caused Holmes no great concern, since we now faced a brick wall.

“A dead-end, Watson. He cannot be far away.” To the driver, he said. “You have done well. If you would care to wait for us again, you will enhance your fare even further. I do not anticipate that we will be long.”

The man assented and we left the hansom quietly, walking back past several pairs of iron gates. I could see no way of telling which of these the cart had entered, but Holmes seemed absorbed in studying the locks and would, I am sure, have somehow found our way, had not the stamping of an impatient or hungry horse alerted us. We remained still and listened, until the dull impacts of iron shoes upon the stones were repeated. Holmes said nothing, but opened one of the gates slowly when it proved to be unlocked.

Once inside, we listened again and heard nothing. We crept slowly between two buildings, into a small courtyard. There the cart stood, with the horse tied to a broken pipe projecting from a crumbling wall. A wide door, used no doubt for deliveries, stood half-open before us.

"Are you armed, Watson?" Holmes whispered.

"My hand is on my service revolver."

"Excellent. I see that there is a light within."

We entered slowly, making no noise, and stood in the shadows near the door. The room was dimly lit by two oil lamps mounted on overturned storage crates, and smelled disgustingly. Holmes indicated that we should do nothing for the moment, until we understood the scene before us, but the need for action was apparent.

The man I assumed to be Warrilow stood with his back to us, facing two people who were each manacled by one arm to the wall. The girl, who was clearly Martha Redstrap, was in a pitiable state. She leaned against her chains with her clothes torn and filthy. A few feet away an unshaven man stood defiantly but in obvious distress, and in a similar condition. In full view of the prisoners but, I estimated, just out of their reach, stood an upturned box laden with a bottle of water and a loaf of mouldy bread.

"You are an obstinate man, Northbridge," Warrilow said. "You will get no more water or bread until you tell me how much Scotland Yard knows of our plans. Much has been risked for what is to come, and we cannot tolerate interference." He turned to the girl, and I felt Holmes grow tense beside me. "Perhaps some attention to Miss Redstrap, whose father has been most co-operative, will loosen your tongue."

He tore the girl's dress half from her body, with a quick sweep of his arm.

"Leave her!" Northbridge shouted. "She cannot harm your plans."

"That is true," Warrilow agreed. "In fact, she has served her purpose well. Her father has surrendered the plans of the bank vaults and I have promised to return her to him. As a gentleman, it grieves me not to keep that promise."

He said it with a mocking lack of sincerity, and it brought a mixture of anger and despair to Northbridge's face. "So that has become your intention?"

"That was always my intention."

"Then that is another reason why I shall tell you nothing."

Warrilow laughed. "You think that is how it will be? I tell you that long before you depart this life you will be glad to pour out your soul to me."

Holmes stepped forward and new hope flared in Northbridge's eyes. Warrilow saw it at once and turned to face us. Surprise came and faded from his face quickly.

"Well, Mr Sherlock Holmes. Such a surprise to see you here."

"We are here to escort you to Scotland Yard, Warrilow. There can be no escape this time."

Warrilow glanced calmly about him, as if searching for a weapon or a means of escape. With a shrug he walked slowly towards us, his wrists held out to invite Holmes to place handcuffs upon them. I had remained in deep shadow and he was not yet aware of my presence. My friend stood very still as Warrilow approached, and I had an impression of a heavily moustached face with cruel eyes, advancing in the semi-darkness.

Then, with the quickness of a fairground conjuror, one of the offered hands disappeared inside the pea jacket he wore. It came out raised to strike, ready to plunge a long knife into the chest of Sherlock Holmes.

My friend had already evaded the thrust as I fired. The sound seemed as loud as a cannon in the enclosed space, and Warrilow was hurled backwards and toppled to the floor. The girl screamed as he fell near her, and I put away my revolver and stood over him. I saw at once that there was nothing that could be done to save him. His filthy shirt was moist with blood, and more dribbled from his mouth as he coughed.

"He will get you," he gasped painfully. "You will see."

His eyes went blank and he expired with a deep sigh.

"Thank you, Watson, though your action was a little premature."

"He would have killed you, Holmes!"

"So it must have appeared to you, but I had already avoided the blade. Unfortunately, we can learn nothing from him now."

Feeling rather hurt by my friend's attitude, I retrieved a bunch of keys from Warrilow's pockets and handed them to him. Both prisoners were quickly released, and I fetched fresh water from a tap in an adjoining room for them. Martha Redstrap covered herself with a tattered blanket that I discovered in an otherwise empty crate, while Northbridge sat down to regain his strength.

Holmes drew something from his pocket. "Watson, here is a police whistle. Pray be good enough to walk to both ends of the street and blow it until a constable appears. That should not take long, since the beats hereabouts are designed to intersect every fifteen minutes. Meanwhile, I will attend to our charges as best I can."

I was back with two constables within twenty minutes. Holmes explained the situation, mentioning that Inspector Lestrade's enquiries were connected also. One officer left to summon a sergeant, while the other remained. It was understood that Inspector Northbridge and Miss Martha Redstrap would be escorted to hospital for observation, that her father would be notified of her safe recovery and that the body of Warrilow would be conveyed to the nearest mortuary.

Our driver received a generous payment on returning us to Baker Street, and seemed well pleased. It was past five o'clock as we regained our sitting room. Strangely, neither Holmes or myself felt undue weariness as we sat either side of an unlit fire watching the new day grow lighter.

"A good night's work I think, Holmes." I remarked as I put down my empty glass.

"Indeed. Watson, I must thank you again for attempting to save my life. You must have thought me most ungrateful at the time."

“Not at all, old fellow. I understand that I unwittingly deprived us of information.”

“You realise then, that this affair is not over?”

I nodded. “Warrilow referred to someone who he expected to take revenge on us. Also, there remain unanswered questions regarding Inspector Northbridge.”

“Your deductive powers improve by leaps and bounds,” he said, and I felt warm satisfaction at his praise. “While you summoned the constables I talked at length to Northbridge, having first discharged the distressing task of informing him of his mother’s death. His enquiries had revealed the connection between Warrilow, whom he was certain to be responsible for the previous two murders, and Mr Redstrap of the Agricultural & Landowners Bank. I did in fact confirm Warrilow’s guilt, by examining the thin chain that he kept about his waist. The shape of the links was identical to the impressions on the victims’ throats.”

“But Mr Redstrap was afraid for his daughter’s life and so concealed the situation, as he attempted to with us.”

“Precisely. Warrilow somehow became aware of the pursuit, probably Mr Redstrap volunteered it accidentally, subsequently captured Northbridge and murdered Northbridge’s mother for fear of what might have been disclosed to her. He kept the Inspector alive in order to learn how much Scotland Yard knew about the forthcoming crimes. I found two draughtsman’s drawings in that warehouse, and one of them is clearly of Mr Redstrap’s bank.”

“And the other?” I asked.

Holmes plucked two thick documents from the table, and discarded one of them. The other he unfolded, glanced at it and held it so that I could see the diagram drawn upon it.

“A building meant to contain a large number of people, I think.” He observed.

“There is no writing upon it.”

“And there lies the difficulty.”

I looked more closely. “A hotel, perhaps?”

He frowned, but then his face lit up. “No, Watson, but you gave me the clue. Consider the design, the corridors leading to a central point and the small, regularly-spaced rooms. Can you now throw light upon it?”

For a moment more, I stared. “Of course, it is a map of the inside of a prison!”

“It is indeed. But I see that it is almost fully light out there, and high time that we slept. We will discuss this further over a very late breakfast, but for now I bid you goodnight, or good morning, if you prefer.”

He turned as I rose from my chair, picking up the documents and vanishing into his room abruptly.

The tiredness that I had kept at bay until now suddenly descended upon me. I said goodnight to my friend as I passed his door, yawning as I made my way to my bed.

#

As it happened, neither Holmes or myself slept for long. I think I had passed beyond weariness, while he would doubtlessly have remained awake to ponder the remaining problems facing us. My pocket-watch showed almost ten o’clock, as we sat down to a delayed breakfast of bacon and eggs.

Strangely, and contrary to his stated intention of the early morning, my friend said nothing about the case or our discoveries. He ate automatically, maintaining an expression of deep preoccupation except for a few words of greeting.

Mrs Hudson had no sooner cleared away our plates and coffee cups when the door-bell rang. We made ourselves comfortable in our usual armchairs as that good lady showed in Inspector Lestrade and withdrew.

"Lestrade!" Holmes called out in a surprisingly jovial manner. "Come and sit with us. Watson, pray be good enough to call down to Mrs Hudson for another pot of coffee."

"Not for me, if you don't mind, Mr Holmes", the little detective responded. "For once, I've managed to have breakfast before beginning my duty."

I remained seated therefore, and Lestrade settled himself in the empty chair.

"I came to discuss this Warrilow business of course," he said. "I read the constable's report about the events of last night."

"How are Inspector Northbridge and Miss Martha Redstrap?" I enquired, despite Holmes' obvious annoyance at my interruption.

"They are recovering well, as far as I know. Miss Redstrap has been returned to her parents."

"Excellent," said Holmes, by way of dismissing the subject. "I have recovered a plan of the bank, from Warrilow. Is there any reason why a robbery should have been planned at this particular time, Lestrade?"

"The Yard has been informed that an excessive amount of bullion is on hand, to repay a number of international loans."

“That would certainly account for it. There was also another document, which Watson and I have identified as a map of the interior of a prison. Is it, by any chance, familiar to you?”

Lestrade scowled as my friend handed him the document, and I knew this was because we had removed articles from the scene, unofficially. He leaned forward to spread it out before him and gave us a sharp glance. “I have seen this before now. It is indeed a map of Pentonville Prison. You say it was recovered from Warrilow?”

Holmes had become very still, and appeared to be deep in thought. He did not answer the inspector’s question, but said suddenly: “The telegram I sent to you yesterday evening, Lestrade. Did you receive it?”

“I was away from The Yard until late. I must have missed it when I called in briefly, this morning. What did it contain?”

“An enquiry about the professions of Warrilow’s two previous victims.”

“The first, Stephen Mortimer, was an ex-clerk from the very same bank, until he was dismissed for suspected dishonesty. No doubt Warrilow learned much from him, about the bank and the Redstrap family, before the murder. I imagine he surrendered the information after a promise of payment.”

“Undoubtedly. But the second victim?”

I saw Lestrade’s face go pale as he realised the implication of what he was about to say.

“Frederick Purcell was a guard at Pentonville Prison. Warrilow must have used him similarly, to obtain this plan and possibly information also.”

“And Warrilow’s last words were to the effect that an accomplice of his would take revenge on us.”

“So there is more yet to this business,” the little detective realised. “The intentions were to rob the bank, and then break into the prison?”

Holmes declined to answer, but asked. “Is anyone of particular notoriety held there at present?”

“There is indeed, as of yesterday. The Fallon gang, four men of a black-hearted family who have eluded us until now are to be brought to trial for a number of murders and armed robberies. You believe there is some connection, Mr Holmes?”

“I suspect that the entire sequence of events is connected,” my friend replied. “The bank robbery is a distraction device, intended to engage the attention of Scotland Yard while the real crime, the releasing from prison of the Fallon Gang, is to be perpetrated. I think the two events, with Warrilow as the common factor, could not be otherwise. From this we see at once, that not only must we do our utmost to discover when these acts are to be carried out, but that it is imperative that the true account of Warrilow’s death be concealed. The fact that this gang, whoever they may be, are prepared to take so much trouble to extract these men from custody suggests that a much more elaborate crime awaits their participation in the near future. Something to watch for, Lestrade.”

“We will, never fear. But why should the cause of Warrilow’s death be hidden?”

“Because, if it were known that Watson and myself, or indeed any member of the official force, were involved, the gang would be warned that we know of their intentions and probably change them. I suggest that the newspapers are told that Northbridge and Miss Redstrap escaped, without having learned anything of value to Scotland Yard, and that Warrilow was killed as he tried to prevent this. Both sets of plans will have to be replaced where they were found of course, if it is not too late."

"No information about the incident has yet been released," the Scotland Yard man confirmed thoughtfully.

"Then we can proceed. For now, it will be a waiting game."

#

Nothing was heard for a week. When I commented on this, Holmes explained that this did not necessarily mean that the gang had changed its plans, since they would have to choose a replacement to take Warrilow's part in the assault on the bank and to finalise and co-ordinate the two operations. I asked if there was a possibility of an error in the construction of his theory, and my friend looked up from his newspaper with an icy glare.

"Warrilow had both sets of plans, therefore the two crimes are connected. Even if I believed in coincidence, Watson, that would be too much. Besides, this case has other features of which I will tell you after its conclusion."

For the remainder of that day, and almost all of the next, Holmes languished in that dark mood that always came upon him at times of inactivity. But in the early evening a telegram from Lestrade arrived, bearing the words: Tomorrow. Eight o'clock. This was in accordance with our arrangement, and meant that Scotland Yard had received information that the gang's plans were about to be set in motion.

The little detective was waiting, with fifteen constables armed with truncheons, outside the gates of Pentonville Prison when we arrived at six in the morning. Already, it was fully light and we repaired to the governor's office which overlooked the yard and main gates.

“Mr Redstrap sent a private messenger to the Yard,” Lestrade explained to us, “whose instructions were to deliver the documents he carried into my hands, which he did. They contained a message received by the bank, a reminder to the effect that a new customer, The Credit Bank of Paris, was to deliver a shipment of gold bullion at eight o’clock this morning, before the bank opens. Both the account and the delivery were arranged some weeks ago, before Northbridge disappeared and this affair began, and so no significance was placed upon it, at first. However, in the light of our current suspicions, a telegram was dispatched to Paris for confirmation. This quickly attracted a reply, telling us that they knew of no such account or delivery, and we then established that the London address that the Agricultural & Landowners Bank had dealt with was a barber’s shop where the owner was in the habit of acting as a poste restante for a fee. That was when I arranged for these constables to be in attendance here, and notified you gentlemen as promised.”

“Anticipating the second stage of the gang’s plan,” my friend said with approval. “But what action has been taken to protect the bank?”

“Inspectors Gregson and Bradstreet, accompanied by a dozen armed constables, are ready and waiting.”

“Excellent, Lestrade,” Holmes replied, and at that moment a tall stern-faced man entered and was introduced to us.

“Mr George Wittall, governor of Pentonville.”

He shook hands with us, and his frown deepened. “This is a terrible business, gentlemen. I suppose some violence is inevitable.”

“We are prepared,” said Lestrade. “Myself, Mr Holmes and Doctor Watson, as well as five constables, are armed with revolvers and all constables carry truncheons. Our intention is to keep the disturbance to a minimum, if that proves to be possible."

"Thank you for your consideration. Will you require assistance from the prison staff?"

"Only to bring the Fallon gang into plain view. I understand that you received notification from The Commissioner's Office at Scotland Yard, that these prisoners are required for questioning?"

The governor nodded. "That is quite usual in such circumstances, where a prisoner's involvement to a further, unsolved, crime is suspected."

"And the message appeared to be no different to any other occasion?"

"Not at all."

"Then the gang has an informer at the Yard," Holmes pointed out. "Neither the wording or the presentation of these official messages are known to the general public. One of your colleagues, Lestrade, has been paid or threatened." He paused, and then added: "Such a man could also serve to intercept any request for confirmation from the prison, and to send a reply."

"Could not the information have been forced from Inspector Northbridge?" I ventured.

The little detective shook his head. "Northbridge's duties could not have entailed anything connected with this. I will certainly look into it when I return to my office."

"As recently instructed," the governor finished, "I immediately sought confirmation."

Lestrade then dismissed the man, and our vigil began.

Holmes, Lestrade and I looked down into the prison yard. Before long ten convicts appeared in prison uniform, under the watchful eyes of two armed prison guards. Both of my companions nodded their approval, and I realised then that the party were actually disguised constables. They positioned themselves as if waiting to begin a daily exercise drill, and stood in silence. When two more armed guards emerged from the main building in the company of four heavily-manacled men (I presumed these to be the Fallon gang), Lestrade consulted his pocket watch.

"It is almost time. The remaining three of my men are out of sight and we must take up our positions. The intruders must suspect nothing until the gates are securely fastened, after they enter."

A few minutes after Holmes and I had concealed ourselves in a deep doorway, and Lestrade had found cover behind the projecting brickwork of a chimney, a coach drew up outside the gates. I withdrew my watch from my waistcoat pocket sufficiently to see that the time was exactly eight o'clock.

One of the 'guards' supervising the drill squad approached the gates and peered through the tiny observation port. A short conversation followed, before he shouted that the expected Scotland Yard officers had arrived. I had not seen the governor appear, but he stood near the entrance to the cell block and raised an arm to signal that the gate could be opened. When this was done, a long four-wheeler with police markings entered the yard slowly. The drill squad began its routine.

"This has been exceptionally well-organised," Holmes whispered. "Only a close examination would reveal that not to be an official vehicle."

We watched as the coach came to rest, the driver remaining as he was while two well-dressed men alighted. One, tall and bearded, introduced himself to the governor as 'Inspector Hawkins' while his shorter companion was 'Inspector Turnbull'.

I noticed that the drill squad, and their 'guards', were already advancing slowly towards the coach.

"You will have received notification of this prisoner transfer," Hawkins began when the governor approached. "Here is further authority."

Mr Wittall took the offered documents and spent a few minutes examining their contents. "They appear to be in order," he said.

Hawkins peered past him, at the waiting Fallon gang. "Brutal-looking lot. Still, you've got the derbies and leg-irons on them, so they shouldn't give us any trouble."

Before the governor could reply, one of the Fallon gang, a giant of a man with a scar across his forehead, shouted loudly.

"You are trapped! All is discovered!"

Immediately, chaos burst upon the scene.

Hawkins struck Mr Wittall, producing a revolver from under his long coat as the governor fell. He fired twice at the guards in charge of the prisoners, and one man toppled. The other 'Inspector', Turnbull, leaned into the coach and suddenly there was a shotgun in his hands, and the driver rose from his seat similarly armed. The drill squad had by this time drawn close, and Turnbull fired into their midst. The horses reared in panic, their cries alarmingly loud in the enclosed yard, spoiling the driver's aim and his balance so that he leaped to the ground. He turned in our direction, having apparently sensed our presence, but Lestrade shot him before he could bring his weapon to bear.

Dimly, among the noise and the blood, I was aware of the remaining guard using his truncheon on those of the Fallon gang who resisted his efforts to return them to their cells. Holmes, meanwhile, had shot twice at Hawkins but missed as the man took shelter behind the coach. Fearing fire from the drill squad, he altered his position, and my friend brought him down with a third shot.

For an awful moment there was silence, then Turnbull ran madly towards us. He held his shotgun in his left hand and a revolver in the other aiming indiscriminately at anyone within his sight. A few inches from my head the wall exploded, splattering my face with brick dust. I fired once and he was hurled backwards. He managed to struggle to his knees as the remnants of the drill squad approached, and two disguised constables discharged their weapons until he was still. Then the danger was past and relief swept over us, as one of Lestrade's men calmed the horses, holding their heads.

The smoke from the gun-fire was already dispersing, as I avoided the patches of blood to tend the wounded, obeying the calling of my profession.

#

I asked Mrs Hudson to serve a late lunch, because Holmes had accompanied Lestrade to Scotland Yard.

"How did it go, old fellow?" I asked as he entered our rooms and took off his coat.

"A constable was killed during the bank robbery, Gregson was slightly wounded. All the robbers save one who is badly hurt and under police supervision in hospital, were killed by police gunfire."

"And from Pentonville, finally?"

He shook his head sadly. “Three constables dead, two seriously injured. One guard dead, and one with minor wounds.”

“After a battle of that sort, it could have been much worse, Holmes. How is Mr Wittall?”

“He was unaffected by the shooting. Cuts and bruises from the blow he sustained, nothing more.”

“Our three adversaries were dead, I know. My examination needed to be only superficial.”

“That is a pity. Much could have been learned from them.”

“I thought this business was at an end. Have you discovered something more?”

“I have discovered nothing new,” he said thoughtfully. “that I did not suspect from the beginning.” I was about to ask for an explanation, when he suddenly smiled as the door opened. “But here is Mrs Hudson with our lunch. Poached salmon with new potatoes, I see. We will eat first, Watson, and then retire to our chairs to smoke a pipe, after which I will answer your questions as best I can.”

For once, Holmes proved himself my equal in the consumption of our lunch. He set about his food with unusual enthusiasm, and the meal ended with both our appetites satisfied. When our landlady had cleared away the remains, we took to our armchairs and smoked contentedly.

“I see that your curiosity about this case has not abated over lunch,” he remarked as he knocked out his cherrywood pipe. “Often, Watson, your expression speaks volumes.”

“Only to you, I think.”

"Perhaps, but let me answer your question about what remains of this affair, with a question of my own: do you believe that Warrilow had the guile or the intelligence to plan this two-pronged assault on the resources of Scotland Yard? Remember that there have been an unusual amount of minor crimes committed over the past few weeks, stretching the manpower of the official force considerably."

"Do you suspect that this was a gradual wearing down of the Yard's resources, culminating in these two major crimes?"

"I am quite convinced of it. The intention was that the robbery at the Agricultural & Landowners Bank should not only divert attention from the Pentonville break-out of the Fallon gang, but also that both crimes should take place when the Yard was least able to cope with them."

"I agree, Holmes, that I would not have thought Warrilow capable of such organisation."

"Nor I, and when we assume as much, other aspects of this affair become more credible." He replaced his pipe in the rack and sat back in his chair, his eyes half-closed. "For example, Inspector Northbridge was kept alive, and not immediately disposed of as a threat to the forthcoming criminal operations, inside information was obtained by one device or another, from both the bank and Scotland Yard. Then we have to consider the falsification of credentials from The Credit Bank of Paris, and of those from the Yard. There are many others, Watson, but I think those are sufficient to illustrate the point."

I considered his words, and could not deny the apparent truth in them. "Again, I cannot help but agree. But if Warrilow was a mere instrument in all this as you suggest, then who is truly behind it? Have we been battling with a shadow?"

“That is a more apt description than you realise, old fellow. You may recall that I have remarked to you on several occasions, once in the presence of Inspector MacDonald, that there is an evil influence in London that controls most of the criminal activity that we see around us. I sensed the closeness of his activities to my own some time ago, and have investigated his background. His intelligence is equal to my own, and so he is a formidable enemy. I have no doubts that we shall encounter him in the future.”

www.ingramcontent.com/pod-product-compliance
Lightning Source LLC
LaVergne TN
LVHW050635100826
845148LV00011B/1871

* 9 7 8 1 7 8 7 0 5 6 9 6 1 *